MORE
THAN
MIDNIGHT

MORE
THAN
MIDNIGHT

Short Stories by

BRIAN JAMES FREEMAN

CEMETERY DANCE PUBLICATIONS

Baltimore

2019

For Robert Brouhard

With special thanks to Kathryn for helping me get through these once and for all; to Vicki Liebowitz for the care and feeding along the way; to Norman Prentiss, Serenity Richards, Brad Saenz, Rick Lederman, and Robert Mingee for the ground support; to Gail Cross, Robert Swartwood, and Tabitha Brouhard for the technical support; to Michael Koryta for the inspiring introduction; to Vincent Chong and Glenn Chadbourne for the incredible artwork; and to Richard Chizmar, Brian Keene, Allen Koszowski, Kelly Laymon and Steve Gerlach, and Elizabeth and Tom Monteleone for originally including several of these stories in their publications.

TABLE
OF
CONTENTS

INTRODUCTION

BY MICHAEL KORYTA

DO ME A FAVOR, WOULD you? Dim the lights. Not all the way to darkness, no, we need to leave you a little light. Enough to read by. But just enough.

Because the stories you're about to read aren't designed for beach reading or sunlit afternoons. Not these stories, at least, though I think that Brian can write about anything he wants and make it work.

The stories that lie ahead are designed to put a chill down your spine.

I suspect they will.

Ahead you have a mild-mannered music teacher with a very large blade, a determined wife and mother on her way out of an asylum, phone calls from the dead, and a pair of ruby eyes above a rotting mouth. Some of you sick bastards—like me—are probably already smiling. This is what brought you here, after all, just as if you've pulled the car into a drive-in theater on Halloween night. You're here for scares.

Rest assured, you'll receive them.

You'll also get a little more. As the best writers always do, Brian James Freeman brings more to the table than the simple intent to horrify you with these horror stories. There's clean, sharp prose, there's a compelling, human heart to every tale, fine touches of humor, and an astute understanding of the more powerful emotions in life—terror, sure, but also loss, grief, struggle, endurance.

"I'm not the person I used to be, but I am the person I had to become," Freeman writes in "Among Us."

Freeman is not the writer he used to be—he's better, read *The Painted Darkness* and then tell me I'm wrong—but the writer he has become is the sort of writer I love to see at work in the realm of horror fiction, because he displays a blend of fine writing and a true love for the genre. He's not dabbling with the form, he knows it well, has read and studied and appreciated the best writers, learned from them, and then offered his original voice. The genre is better off for it.

If you're anything like me, you'll feel a kinship to Brian as you read these stories. You'll realize that this is a man who watches something shift in the shadows outside his window and doesn't dismiss it as surely being just the neighbor's dog, a man who hears a chainsaw in the distance and does not assume that its target is a tree.

My kind of guy, in other words. Let his imagination take you along, then. You'll enjoy the trip. But first let's get the atmosphere just right. I'd try to do it myself, but this is Brian's collection, so let's use his words:

THEN LIGHTNING SPLIT THE SKY and the backyard lit up, just for a second.

In the brief moment of blinding clarity, Edward saw the swings blowing wildly in the wind and the tree branches bending down and to the right. The rain beat against the window like a marching band's cadence.

But there was no one there.

FEELING THE RIGHT MOOD YET? I thought so. Carry on, then. Turn the page. And I don't want to spoil anything, but I will tell you this much:

There's someone there.

POP-POP

ERIN AND RUSS STAND WITH their mother in the living room of Gram-Gram's home, surveying their surroundings as if they've never seen this place before. Quite the opposite is true, of course. The twins practically grew up here while their mother worked two jobs to pay the bills. Yet today the house feels different. Somehow it looks different, too, even though nothing obvious has changed.

"She's been having good days and bad days," their mother says for the third time since they left Gram-Gram's cool, sterile room at the Sunny Days Hospice Home. "I'm sorry she had a bad day today."

"Mom, it's okay," Erin says, also for the third time.

"What can we help with?" Russ wants to steer the conversation away from their beloved grandmother's final, confusing weeks. The twins haven't visited with their mother or Gram-Gram very much since they left for college last fall, but now they're home for Easter break and they understand the weight their mother has been carrying all on her own.

"I can't just sit around, waiting for her to..." their mother says, trailing off. "I can't just sit and wait. I need to feel useful, so I guess I'd like to start the prep work to sell the house."

The house. Not Gram-Gram's house, not the house where Gram-Gram and Pop-Pop raised her. Just *the house.* Erin and Russ exchange a look. They haven't taken an intro to psychology class, but they recognize the emotional distancing at play with their mother's choice of words.

She continues, "It'll be tons of work, I mean, but maybe we can start packing a few boxes for Goodwill. What do you kids think?"

"Absolutely, we're game," Erin answers for both of them.

"Great!" Their mother's face lights up a little, just for a second, as if they've decided to plan a surprise party for someone they love instead of preparing her childhood home for sale while an aggressive cancer eats away at her mother.

"We'll start in the attic," Russ says. "There's a lot to sort through."

"Perfect!" their mother replies, once again with too much enthusiasm. "I'll run to the store and get some boxes. Will you kids be okay here by yourselves?"

"Absolutely," Erin and Russ say in unison.

✕

AFTER THEIR MOTHER LEAVES, THE twins make their way up the dusty stairs to the second floor. They both grip the handrail tightly out of habit, not aware of their actions. This was where Pop-Pop slipped and fell one spring day when they were eight years old, breaking his neck at the bottom. He died instantly.

Their mother and Gram-Gram were devastated, and Russ cried on and off for days after the funeral. Pop-Pop had been his favorite person in the entire world.

Yet Erin wasn't particularly sad about the old man's passing, although even at the tender age of eight she knew to keep those thoughts to herself. She had feared Pop-Pop in a way Russ never did. It wasn't that Pop-Pop raised his voice at her or hit her or threatened her or anything awful like that; there was just something off about the way he sometimes looked at her, causing her a sense of unease she couldn't exactly explain or describe. This is not something Erin has ever shared with anyone. What would have been the point once he was gone?

Gram-Gram's decline began right around her husband's death, a connection the twins made as they grew older. First her mobility decreased, then there were serious health scares including a possible stroke, then the memory loss appeared with frightening stealth, and finally the cancer arrived in the night like a thief. It's been a difficult decade for the graceful woman they love so very much.

When the twins reach the second floor, they stop under the familiar attic access. As kids, they discovered they could reach the knotted pull-down cord with the assistance of a chair borrowed from

Gram-Gram's sewing room, and over time they turned the attic into their own little clubhouse. Russ grabs that cord and tugs it toward the floor. The compact ladder unfolds with a shrill screech, and darkness greets them from the opening in the ceiling.

"Do you want to go first or should I?" Russ asks.

"You first. You know I'm a total coward about the dark."

It has been many years and quite a few pounds since Russ last made this climb, and the first wooden rung groans under him. He pauses, confirms the ladder is actually holding his weight, and then continues upward. He vanishes into the dark. The attic's wooden floorboards creak and whine. There's a thud as he trips on something and sends it flying, but before Erin can ask if he's okay, a dull light flickers and fills the opening above her.

"Come on up," Russ calls. "Watch your step, though. It's really bad."

Erin joins her brother in the attic with the sloped ceiling, the musty smell of departed summers, and hundreds of cobwebs dancing in the shadows as spiders vanish into their hiding places. She barely notices these things, which she was expecting, because of what she *wasn't* expecting.

"What happened?"

A dresser has been pushed over and the contents of the drawers are strewn around the dirty floor. Cardboard boxes are overturned and decades worth of paperwork is scattered. The family's ancient board game boxes have been opened and tossed. Two full-length mirrors lay on their sides like fallen soldiers, their glass shattered. Moth-eaten clothes, including Gram-Gram's yellowed wedding dress, are tattered and torn. Framed family portraits and watercolor paintings bought decades ago at Sears & Roebuck have been freed of their frames and ripped into pieces.

Russ says, "Maybe this was one of Gram-Gram's bad days."

"But what was she *doing?*"

"Looking for something, I guess."

"Where do we start?"

"Maybe we'll just gather similar things together, you know? Refold the clothing from the dresser, reassemble the games, that sort of thing."

"Okay," Erin says. "I'll fold the clothing since you couldn't get that right to save your life."

"Hey, I tried folding the laundry once. I didn't see the point. The clothes just get unfolded again. No one wears a folded shirt!"

"Whatever, dork."

They don't say much else while they work, but they're not working in silence, either. The floorboards whimper with every movement and the wind assaults the roof, howling in the eaves. Russ and Erin remember these sounds from when the attic served as their secret playroom, but the space seems so much smaller now—and those sounds are somehow louder and bleaker.

When the dresser has been returned to its rightful place with the contents neatly stored away, the twins begin gathering the components of the board games that landed in every nook and cranny the attic has to offer.

Erin is deep under the sloped roof, nearly to the place where the floor and the ceiling meet, when she stops and ponders something she has spotted.

"Russ," Erin says, "come look at this."

"What's up?" Russ asks, crawling in next to her.

"I saw this piece from the Monopoly game," she says, showing him the little silver rocking horse, "but the head of the horse was stuck between these two floorboards. That's when I realized this board wasn't actually nailed down."

She lifts the board and they peer into the dark space. Russ removes his phone from his pocket, activating the flashlight app. Neither really expects to find anything, other than maybe some dust and more cobwebs, so they're both surprised by the wooden cigar box sitting on top of the lath and plaster ceiling of the bedroom below them.

"What do you think it is?" Russ asks.

"A cigar box, you dork."

"I mean, why's it hidden up here?"

"No idea. Should we open it?"

"Well, who else will?"

Erin nods. She carefully removes the box from where it has been stashed away from prying eyes, wipes at the thick layer of dust, and lifts the lid. Russ positions his phone's light so they can see inside. They stare for a very long time.

"What does it mean?" Erin asks, studying the unexpected contents.

"I'm not sure." Russ removes the school ID cards from inside the cigar box. Most of them are plastic, although they're older than the colorful ID cards Russ and Erin carry, but underneath those are more IDs printed on cardstock, some of which are old enough to only have the student's name, the year, and the school logo.

"Russ... the photos," Erin whispers.

Russ understands, but he cannot find the words to reply. The IDs all belonged to women. Dozens and dozens of women over many decades.

And in many subtle but unmistakable ways, these women resemble how their mother and their Gram-Gram look in photos taken during their late teens and early twenties.

In fact, these women are the spitting image of Erin now.

✕

THE TWINS SIT AT THE kitchen table with the IDs spread across the green tablecloth as if they're playing some kind of card game.

The oldest ID is dated 1967 and the faded information is printed on crumpled card stock, no lamination to protect it. The woman's name is Jennifer Mitchell and the University of Pennsylvania issued the card. The newest one is dated 2007 and the student named Cindy Smith bears such a strong resemblance to Erin that the twins wonder if this woman could somehow be related to them. That ID is from Penn State University and it was issued the year before Pop-Pop fell down the stairs and broke his neck.

"Are you going to do it or am I?" Russ asks.

"I don't think I can."

They're staring at their phones, which sit on the table just out of easy reach as if the devices are unwanted, unloved, even hated. Normally, the phones never leave their hands or pockets, but at this moment they represent a true and present danger to Erin and Russ's understanding of their family and the people they love. With one Internet search, maybe two, their suspicions could be confirmed. They've watched enough reruns of *CSI* and *Criminal Minds* to identify a serial killer's trophy collection when they see it. This search cannot end well, but what else can they do?

"Aw shit," Russ mutters, reaching for his phone. He looks at the most recent ID card and then types the woman's name, her school, and the year into the search bar. Seconds later they have confirmation. He slides the phone over to Erin so she can read it for herself.

"Penn State student Cindy Smith missing for two weeks," she says, glancing from the archived news story to the ID card. "*Harrisburg Patriot News.* April 30, 2008."

She takes the phone and types in the information from the second most recent ID card. Within seconds, those results are conclusive, too. She slides the phone back to her brother.

"Slippery Rock student Amanda Miller still missing one year later," Russ reads. "This story is from the *Butler Eagle,* dated April 25, 2005."

Even though they're certain of what they'll learn, they continue passing the phone back and forth, searching for each woman's name and school. It soon becomes clear the missing women have never been found. Some of the stories are from the tenth or twentieth or thirtieth anniversary of a disappearance. Always in April.

There are countless mentions of loved ones desperately wishing for closure. There are some families who've decided it's better to believe their daughter simply ran away and is living a happy life somewhere. There are wild explanations to rationalize how a person could vanish without a trace. "Maybe she hit her head," suggested the brother of Julie Dean, a Shippensburg University student who went missing while hiking the Appalachian Trail in April of 1987, "and she forgot her name and she's working in a diner somewhere and she don't know she's a missing person."

Erin and Russ understand the truth that Julie Dean's brother and many of the others cannot accept. None of these women are in California trying to make it big, or suffering from amnesia in a small town, or traveling through Europe with a rich prince they met on holiday. These women are dead.

"There are years between some of these, and some were in consecutive Aprils," Russ says.

"Is there a pattern?" Those formulaic crime-solving shows are suddenly coming in handy.

"Not that I can see."

The two siblings are so engrossed by their discovery that they don't hear their mother's car roll into the driveway. If she hadn't locked the kitchen door behind herself, obeying a habit established in early childhood when her father warned her repeatedly about the dangers of the outside world, she would have walked right into the kitchen and seen the ID cards on the table. But there's just enough warning for Russ to slide the cards into a pile and shove them roughly into his pocket.

"Oh, hey kids," their mother says as she enters the kitchen, feigning happiness again. "I bought some boxes. Can you get them out of the car for me?"

"Yes!" Erin and Russ answer in unison.

They do their best to act normal for the rest of the day, not giving their mother any indication of the awful knowledge they possess, but she still asks them several times if they're all right.

They say yes, of course, right as rain. What could possibly be wrong?

✕

WHEN THE ELEVATOR DOORS SLIDE open, Erin and Russ step into the bright and deceitfully cheery hallway of the fourth floor of the Sunny Days Hospice Home. Their previous visit with Gram-Gram the day before feels like a million years ago. Their shoes seem too heavy, squeaking loudly on the buffed floor. A television blares an episode of *Jeopardy* from one room, but most of the other rooms are silent.

"Are you *really* going to ask her?" Russ whispers.

"We have to *try* to ask her."

"But it's Pop-Pop. He never acted nuts, you know? How could he be a killer?"

"That's what I want to find out." Erin's tone is familiar to anyone in the family. She's made up her mind and nothing can change it.

When the twins arrive at the end of the hallway, Russ has a flash of intuition. Gram-Gram will be dead. Her cooling corpse will be slumped in her bed, highlighted by a beam of sunlight pouring in through the window. He and Erin will be devastated, of course, but they also won't have to ask about their grandfather's horrific hobby—and maybe that'll be a blessing.

His intuition is wrong, though.

When Erin knocks and pushes the door open, Gram-Gram is very much alive. Her eyes are closed and she *is* in a sunbeam as he imagined, but she's sitting in the chair by the window. The sunlight washes across her pale, gray, wrinkled face. She's dressed in a cloth gown and her deflated chest rises and falls.

Yesterday, she couldn't leave the bed and the words she hissed reminded Russ of *The Exorcist*. He has never tried to talk Erin into watching that one, even though he loves to frighten her with horror films. She scares easily. Yet, here she is, being the brave one, ready to ask her unaskable questions.

"Gram-Gram?"

"Oh my," Gram-Gram replies, opening her eyes and turning her head. Her eyes are blue and sharp, not the cloudy and confused orbs the twins saw the day before. "Erin? Russell? Oh, it's so good to see you! You're getting so big!"

"Hi, Gram-Gram," Russ says, forcing himself to speak.

"Please sit." She gestures toward the visitor chairs pushed against the wall under a flat-screen television.

Her chair can swivel and she uses her bony feet to glide herself around to face them. The sunlight makes her glow as if she's more alive than ever, yet even in the radiance of one of her good days the twins recognize how little is left of her.

"How are you? How is school? Not fucking around too much, I hope?"

Her voice is the same as they remember, but the words aren't. The woman they've loved all their lives would never use profanity, but their mother has warned them that Gram-Gram's mental filters are gone and she has shocked her own daughter several times by unleashing the crass language she apparently kept locked inside her head for most of her life.

"School is great," Erin replies without missing a beat. "Gram-Gram, how are *you* feeling?"

"Oh, I might be having a good day, truth be told," their grandmother says, her coffee-colored teeth showing in a crooked smile on her too-thin face. She gives them a comically burlesque wink. "Haven't had many of those lately. Oh, I'm just so happy to see you both! Is your mother here?"

"Mom doesn't know we came. Russ and I... we have to ask you about something."

"Oh, what's that?"

Erin glances at Russ and he removes the ID cards from his pocket, his trembling fingers nearly dropping them to the floor. He holds them out for their grandmother to see more easily. Her eyes blink and focus. The smile fades and Russ cannot place the new expression that appears briefly on her face and vanishes just as quickly. Guilt, maybe?

"You found those goddamned mementos? Well, I'm glad it was you! Someone needed to and my brain is turning to mush and I couldn't. I searched everywhere. Good for you, kids. Good for you."

"But Gram-Gram, how could anyone do something so awful?" Erin asks.

"It's hard to explain, I'm afraid. Pop-Pop and I had so many fights about that damn ritual and yet I still don't truly understand. Each year April would roll around and if the weather was nice...

well, things just kind of happened. Once the dirty business was taken care of, life went back to normal. But can you imagine the talk if the neighbors found out? Every year I'd pray for an ugly April. Then the *nastiness* wouldn't happen at all! But some years April would be pretty and sunny and fuck me it's a miracle the police never came knocking on our door. Not once!"

"But those young women..." Erin's voice trails off as the question dies in her throat.

"Yes, dreadful, fucking dreadful. Their families will never have closure and I feel terrible about that. Your Pop-Pop and I argued many times about doing *something* to help, maybe mailing anonymous letters to the families. One of our fights actually got a little too heated and down the steps Pop-Pop went! I wish he hadn't, but he did, and I guess now you know the truth about his death, which is right, I believe. You should know. Maybe don't tell your mother, though!"

Erin and Russ are stunned into silence. They stare at their grandmother, who is smiling and speaking of horrible things they never imagined possible when they drove home from college just twenty-four hours ago. Nothing feels real, nothing feels right. Not their thoughts and not their world, which they are seeing with cynical new eyes.

"But Gram-Gram," Russ finally says, "*Why* did Pop-Pop kill *those* young women?"

Their grandmother's lips twitch and her eyes fog a bit, glazing over like they did yesterday. Russ fears she's slipping back into the place she goes on her bad days, but then her eyes brighten and that odd expression passes across her face again, the one he saw when she first gazed at the ID cards. It wasn't guilt at all, he realizes. It was *pride*.

"Oh dearie," she whispers with a sly grin, "Not Pop-Pop."

ANSWERING THE CALL

THE YOUNG MAN MUST BE lonely.

There is something terrible about the look in his eyes, about the way his body slumps over the heavy, black answering machine perched on his lap. He sits on the chair in the middle of the barren room, and he is naked except for his white underwear and his cheap watch. He's drenched in sweat. A single tear hovers on the edge of his pale, trembling lips. He has dark hair and narrow fingers with fingernails chewed to the quick.

The wood floor groans when he shifts his weight. There are no windows, only the door to the hallway and a door to the walk-in closet. A single lamp glows with a yellowed light, but the light does not reach the corners of the room. An extension cord snakes across the floor, powering the lamp and the old, boxy answering machine.

He pushes the button that was once marked ANNOUNCEMENT before years of contact rubbed the word away. The tape crackles, there is a beep, and a woman's voice speaks: "You've reached the Smith Family, we can't come to the phone right now, but if you leave a message, we'll get right back to you."

This is the voice of the dead. The sound has deteriorated a bit with age, but when the young man plays this tape, the dead woman lives on, just for a moment. There is a second beep and the woman is dead once again.

The young man plays the tape one last time, then checks his watch and sighs. He returns the machine to the closet. He wouldn't want to be late for work, and the dead woman isn't going anywhere.

THE YOUNG MAN WALKS WITH a purpose through the high-class neighborhood. There's no hurry, but he is punctual to a fault when it comes to his work. In his pocket is a special digital recorder and a selection of small tools he has found useful on past jobs.

The houses are old and refined yet clearly updated with the most modern conveniences. Hedges and wrought iron fences border the properties, but the gate to his destination is already open to accept guests. He approaches the enormous front door and hammers the golden knocker with a quick slap.

An older woman answers. She is wearing a black dress, and she's been crying. Of course. They usually cry.

He says: "Hello, ma'am, I'm Mr. Smith. I'm from the funeral home."

"Oh, yes, they said you'd come," she replies, her voice distant, as if she isn't aware of what she's saying. The young man understands. A death in the family can be a serious shock to the system, sending a person's world completely out of orbit. She says: "My name is Margaret. Do you need anything from me?"

"No, ma'am. I'm here to help you. Please know that you have my most sincere sympathy for your loss."

She only nods, barely even seeing him.

X

TWENTY MINUTES LATER, THE WOMAN and her family have left for the funeral.

The young man sits with a phone at the marble island in the center of the spacious kitchen. His presence is meant to deter thieves who might have seen the obituary in the newspaper and decided this would be a good time for a break-in. It's a more common occurrence than most people realize, and often the criminals call first, just to make sure the house is empty.

When the doorbell echoes through the house, the young man makes his way to the three-story foyer with the marble floor, crystal chandelier, and dozens of flower arrangements. The house is very beautiful, but very cold.

He answers the door and accepts more flowers from the delivery driver who greedily eyes the inside of the majestic home. When the delivery van cruises away, the young man stands outside longer than necessary, just to be seen. He scours the neighborhood for anyone monitoring the property. There is no one.

After he closes and bolts the door, he places the flowers on the table and carefully proceeds up the curved staircase.

It's time to do what he really came here to do. His real job.

There is a hallway on the third floor. European paintings line the walls. Definitely old. Possibly originals. They do not concern him.

At the end of the hallway is a locked door.

The young man approaches, removes a tool from his pocket, easily picks the lock, and steps inside.

The floors are polished wood. There is a wide mahogany desk and a dozen bookshelves full of leather-bound books. Thousands of them.

There are no windows.

The room is very, very cold.

The young man crosses the home office and studies the desk, which is neatly organized. There is an old phone with an answering machine on the corner. He won't need the special digital recorder in his pocket, which he's used more often than not lately. So few people have real answering machines these days.

A chill crawls along the young man's spine, poking at him with icy fingers.

This isn't right, he thinks.

He's done this many times, but he's never felt this way before. Perspiration forms on his brow. His nerves scream at him to flee. Yet what can he do? He came here to do a job and there's no leaving until it is done.

When he sits behind the desk, the coldness that started in his spine spreads to his arms and legs, chilling his blood. His head throbs. He feels a sensation like a dagger shoving its way through his skull and into his brain. The pain is simple, precise, and extraordinary.

He wants to run from the office, to run all the way home, but it's too late for that. He will be here until his task is completed or until he's dead, whichever comes first.

The phone on the desk rings.

A scream pierces his mind, making him throw his head back, open his mouth wide and join in. Invisible hands restrain his arms, but he *must* answer the phone. If he doesn't, he will die and the family who lives here will never be safe. No one will ever be safe in this place again.

He struggles with all his might, breaks free and grabs for the phone. Still those unseen hands fight for control. Both of the young man's sleeves simultaneously shred from wrist to shoulder as if the seams have been yanked in a million directions at once. He can see the blue on his pale flesh where fingers are again wrapping around his bony arm, trying to prevent him from answering the call. His watch is ripped away and sent flying across the room.

The young man screams, focusing all of his energy and talent and knowledge, and he breaks free yet again. He gets the phone to his ear and pushes the RECORD button on the answering machine at the same time.

"Hello," he says, and there is a roar like a thundering train in a tunnel as images rush past his eyes, searing into the soft tissues of his brain where the ice pick sensation only grows worse.

He sees:

A woman in 1930s Germany being tied to a bed and raped by her teenage son and his friends; children in a concentration camp suffocating as the poison gas collapses their lungs while a guard watches, surprised by his own arousal; a little girl in Argentina, bloody and dead in a filthy alley; a bride's "accidental" slip and fall in the shower after she nervously laughed at her new, older husband's failure to perform on their wedding night; a young boy, strangled to death on the banks of a river near a famous American city; more dead girls, more dead boys, so many dead children over the years, all over the world; and finally the deceased's chance encounter with a woman named Margaret, a woman who in time learned his terrible secrets and didn't care.

The young man feels the fingers of the dead man push between his lips, grabbing at his tongue, pinching and pulling.

The young man gags and he screams into the phone as those bony hands wrap around his throat again:

"Blessed be the people who dwell within this residence and may they be free of your furious spirit when they sleep within these walls that I bless in the name of Jesus, of Buddha, of Mohammed, of Manitou, of Acolnahuacatl, of Thanatos, and may the people of the world of the living be free of your residual presence as you shall be banished to the tape in this Earthly machine while your mortal frame is interned to the ground forever!"

The hands drop from the young man's burning throat, the icy dagger withdraws from his brain, and the room begins to warm, ever so slightly.

MUCH LATER, THE YOUNG MAN sits in his chair in his barren room under the yellowed light of the lamp and he holds the new answering machine.

He is very pale and sweaty, beaten and broken, but he's finished his work yet again.

There are burns on his body from the hands and fingers of the deceased, but he doesn't bother to look. The wounds are part of the job.

The woman named Margaret and all others who live in that house will be safe from the fury of the dead.

At least until Margaret dies. The young man has a bad feeling about her.

He presses the PLAY button on the newest addition to his collection.

The room's walls hear a thick German voice say: "You've reached the private line of Mister VonMueller, please leave a message and I'll get back to you as soon as possible."

But the young man doesn't hear those words.

Instead, he hears a strident version of that same voice screaming: "I'LL KILL YOU, *HURENSOHN,* YOU LITTLE MUTHAFUCKER, YOU LITTLE *STÜCK SCHEIße, VERDAMMTE SCHEIße,* IF YOU DON'T LEAVE THIS PLACE NOW, AND I MEAN RIGHT NOW..."

The recording goes on like that for almost seven minutes.

The young man had no idea it took him so long to say the required words after he answered the phone, but time is funny when he's doing his job.

The tape plays on, and eventually the words of the deceased slur from German profanities into the language only the dead understand until, near the end, there is the young man's chant, over and over again, and then nothing else until the jarring beep as the recording ends.

He turns off the machine, slides off the chair, and opens the door to the closet.

He steps inside.

The closet extends for as far as he can see. There are hundreds of doors in this endless hallway. Lining the walls of the hall, from floor to ceiling, are answering machines of every make and model ever made, along with boxes and boxes of digital tapes and thumb drives. There are millions, perhaps billions of devices containing the words and spirits of the dead.

The young man walks until he finds an open slot where he adds Mister VonMueller to the collection. Then he returns to his room.

He occasionally sees other people entering and exiting from the other doors, but he is forbidden from talking to them, and that's just one of the reasons why the young man is lonely as hell.

But that's not the *only* reason. He's exhausted and he can't imagine spending the rest of his days ridding the world of evil. There's just so much of it. More and more every minute, every hour, every day. Is that really why he was put on this Earth?

The young man doesn't think so, and he wishes he knew his true purpose. He wishes he weren't so alone all the time.

He thinks maybe there's another call to answer in life.

The dead are dead, after all.

They shouldn't have so much control over his life.

Someday, the young man hopes to be free of this terrible responsibility.

Someday very soon.

But for now there are the dead, just waiting for their chance to return to the world of the living, and he has a job to do.

THE FINAL LESSON

RONALD HAMMERSTEIN COULD FEEL SOMEONE watching him as he mowed the lawn in front of his home. The sun was slipping behind the mountains to the west, but just a few more passes and he would be done. Good timing, too, because the bagger on the push mower was nearly full.

The sensation of being watched was unnerving, though. The scrawny little man wiped the sweat from his forehead as he searched the tree-lined street for who might have eyes on him. Normally this was a quiet neighborhood, a nice place to live. The homes were well cared for and he often heard the laughter of children playing in the nearby park, especially in the summer. He wasn't very social, but he liked his neighbors. They were good people.

Maybe that was why he hadn't bolted to start a new life somewhere else, even though the urge had been strong, especially in the months after his wife's death. Some days he still felt like jumping in his car and leaving everything behind, but he couldn't make himself do it. Deep down he knew the loneliness wouldn't be any better somewhere else.

All Ronald had left in this world to care about was his home and his students at work, and both places were haunted by memories both sweet and troubling. He and Jennifer had met as teachers at the Community School—he taught music, she English. At first, they had just casually chatted in the break room during their shared planning period, but those chats grew longer and more in-depth, and soon courtship followed and a year later they were happily married.

Then, two years ago, Jennifer had been brutally stabbed to death in the side parking lot of the Stop-N-Go mini-mart on the state road that connected their community to the Turnpike. It was late at night, the store was the only one in their sleepy little town still open, and she was there to purchase cough medicine for Ronald. She had been stabbed more than one hundred times. Her purse was slashed open and her wallet was taken.

There were no witnesses and the store's outside security camera had been busted. Because she was on the side of the building away from the large glass front windows, her body had laid there next to her car for nearly two hours before a townie with insomnia and the munchies found her. Ronald had fallen asleep while waiting for his wife to return and didn't know anything was wrong until the sheriff knocked on his door.

The sheriff had quickly ruled Ronald out as a suspect and focused the investigation on a White Whippet Bus that was at the Stop-N-Go around the same time, but many of the passengers had paid cash and there was no official passenger manifest, so once everyone went their separate ways in Pittsburgh, which happened before anyone knew Jennifer was dead, it was hard to figure out who had been there.

The entire community mourned with Ronald, of course. An emotional prayer service was held in the school auditorium and a makeshift memorial was created in the gardens. A permanent bronze plaque would eventually be placed there among the flowers. Engraved upon it was one of Jennifer's favorite quotes about why she had become a teacher: *If even one of my lessons changes a student's life for the better, then I will have succeeded.*

Eventually, though, when it became clear the killer probably wouldn't be caught, probably wasn't a local—*couldn't* be a local because only a monster would have done this sort of thing—interest waned, as if the murder had been a bad dream.

People still consoled Ronald on his loss, two years later, but they didn't seem to *really* remember how his wife had been ripped from his perfect little world. They spoke as if she had somehow just faded away.

For everyone except Ronald, life had settled down again. Everyone had returned to feeling safe and secure in their quiet little town.

At least until this morning.

THE FINAL LESSON

The murder of the Derrick couple had the community visibly shaken again. This was a small town in western Pennsylvania, after all, not Pittsburgh or Philly or even Harrisburg. What had been done to the kindly old couple was cold-blooded and horrific, and their deaths had hit Ronald especially hard because he knew them so well.

They were well-respected and beloved teachers at the Community School, and had been for many years, and they were brutalized for an entire night by their attacker. The crime wasn't just murder, it was much, much worse. What had been done to them was inhuman.

Ronald couldn't stop thinking about how their bodies had been found, which was one reason he had decided to do something to keep himself busy, but now he stopped again. That feeling of being watched grew stronger. Invisible icy fingers caressed his spine and he shuddered. Maybe he was just giving in to paranoia, but something didn't seem right. He had barely seen any of his neighbors this evening, as if everyone were staying inside. Maybe, given what happened to the Derricks, they were smart to do so.

He hurried to mow the last strip of grass between the sidewalk and the street, and then he killed the engine and pushed the mower toward his garage where he would empty the bagger into a heavy-duty garbage bag. He wanted to get inside as fast as he could, but the closer he got to the house, the stronger the feeling of being watched became.

Then he realized why. Someone was in the garage, deep in the shadows. Ronald tried to summon his courage, but he wasn't a brave man by nature. He wanted to call out, to make some threat that would scare the person into showing himself. Yet he couldn't think of anything to say, and even if he *did* say something threatening, who would be afraid of a scrawny music teacher?

Ronald opened his mouth, but still no words came. His throat wouldn't allow him to make any sounds. He forced himself to cough and he managed to squeak out a question that wouldn't have scared a mouse:

"Who... Who's in there?"

More movement in the shadows, but no answer. The sun was nearly gone and he wished he had started mowing earlier in the day or maybe just stayed inside like everyone else with a lick of common sense apparently had. There was no one to be seen anywhere on the street. Nobody would be coming to his rescue.

"Who's in there?" he asked again, his voice uneven, cracking with each word.

Two teenagers dressed all in black emerged from the shadows. Their rough leather jackets were ragged with holes. Dog collars lined with metal spikes hugged their necks and they wore heavy military boots. One of them was tall, the other short. At first Ronald thought the tall teen had two black eyes, but then he realized the marks were tattoos.

"How's it hanging, Ronnie McDonnie?" the tattooed teen asked.

"Why are you in my garage?"

"We just wanna chat with ya," the shorter teen said.

He grinned, but the expression formed on his face in such a disturbing, awkward manner that Ronald took a step backwards. He knew he had to get away from these two, he understood they meant trouble, but he wasn't sure how he could do that. They were blocking his path through the garage, and if he tried to make his way to the front door, either one of them would be able to run him down if they wanted to do so. He decided he would have to use his words and simple logic to get them to stop trespassing.

"If you boys leave, I won't have to call the cops."

Both teens looked at each other, eyes wide and bugging out comically, and then they laughed. Their cackles were feral, uncontrolled. The sound started guttural and low but grew louder and more shrill. The taller teen bent over and slapped his knee like he had just heard the funniest joke of his life. Then he straightened back up, pretended to wipe a tear from his eye, and looked at the music teacher with cold, merciless eyes that showed no humor at all.

"You just think you're The Man, dontcha Ronnie?"

"Listen, I don't want any trouble..."

"No! *You* listen to *us*. We came here for a reason, and we're going to get what we want."

THE FINAL LESSON

"I don't have any cash..." Ronald started to say, but before he could finish, the teens reached into their pockets and pulled out knives, which were gleaming and sharp.

"We don't want your cash, dumbass," the short teen whispered. "We want your blood."

As the sun vanished behind the mountains and darkness claimed the world for another night, Ronald realizes these two had killed the Derricks. The fact was as simple as it was horrifying. They had raped and skinned the couple alive and then left their bodies hanging upside down from the flagpole at the Community School for the entire town to see, blood dripping and pooling in the grass.

Ronald's stomach tightened as hot liquid rushed up his throat. He bent over next to his lawn mower and vomited. He couldn't help himself. Fear filled him, draining the strength from his arms and legs.

The tattooed teen smiled crookedly. "Yeah, you recognize our handiwork, do you? Those old fucks were fun to cut. Oh yeah, we cut them good. We should've played with your wife like that, Ronnie McDonnie."

Ronald wiped the vomit from his lips and stared in horror as comprehension dawned. He thought of his wife lying on the pavement of the Stop-N-Go as a blade penetrated her side again and again, her blood flowing out into the night. She had gasped her last bloody gulps of air while he was home sick on their couch, completely unware and useless. Sometimes, during long nights spent alone in their bedroom, he could almost hear her gurgling cries for help.

"Ronnie McDonnie, don't you know who we are?"

Even through his confusion, Ronald realized he *did* remember these two. And why shouldn't he? They had been his students... until... until what?

"You failed our asses and so did your bitch," the tattooed teen said. "We dropped out, just to piss everyone off! You all said we'd go nowhere, but oh, the places we've gone."

Ronald knew their names. He had failed so few students that he easily remembered them. They had been in his Basic Music Theory class the year before Jennifer died. They had put no effort into the class, none at all. Yet if they hadn't been so determined to bully the kids they called sluts and fags, Ronald probably would have let them pass anyway. He didn't like seeing students fail. But these two had gone too far and he just couldn't justify letting them slide, not even with a D.

Not that any of it mattered: not their names, not the horrible things they called the other students, none of it. All that mattered was the evil glimmer in their eyes and the knives in their hands.

The tattooed teen raised his blade a little. It sparkled in the light of the rising moon.

"We used the cash we got from your bitch to take the bus to the city. Pittsburgh is great, man, it really is. We've met a lot of people, made a lot of deals, and we're bringing it all back here. We've got some good shit the school kids are gonna love! First, though, we had to get our payback, know what I mean? Gotta settle some scores and make things right."

"Why'd... why'd you kill the Derricks?"

"Well, duh, they failed our asses, just like you did. They're dead, boo hoo, so sad, and now we want to see you die all curled up like a baby and cryin' for your momma just like your bitch."

"Stop it," Ronald whispered. "Stop it."

"We'll stop when we're ready to stop, Mr. Man. Everyone in this goddamned shit town thinks their shit don't stink, but we're gonna teach all you a lesson. Everyone's gonna fuckin' regret treating us like trailer trash shit."

Ronald's heart was pounding so hard he could barely hear anything else. He thought of his wife dying on the warm pavement of the Stop-N-Go. He thought of the skinned couple hanging from the flagpole at the school, their blood pooling under their naked and violated bodies. He wanted to scream.

"Hey Ronnie McDonnie," the shorter teen said. "You still in there, man? You're looking a little pale."

"Stop it," Ronald whispered again. It seemed to be all he *could* say.

"You know what, Ronnie, for old time's sake, we'll make it a fair fight," the tattooed teen said as he tossed his knife at the music teacher's feet. "There ya go. It's the bigger blade."

Ronald stared at the knife on the edge of his driveway, next to his puddle of vomit and his lawn mower, which he had completely forgotten about, as if mowing the lawn was something he had done in another lifetime.

He thought again about his wife and the Derricks and what a nice town this used to be.

He thought about how these two little monsters had destroyed his life by taking Jennifer away from him, how they were now planning to destroy his community with murder and drugs and God knew what else from the big city.

Ronald's outright horror transformed into a new emotion he hadn't truly experienced before in his entire life.

Rage rose inside of him like a towering gasoline-fueled inferno.

He had never been in a fight in his entire life—he had never raised his fist in anger—but he wanted to *kill* these boys.

He wanted to make them pay for what they had done.

The blinding fury consumed him from out of nowhere.

These two weren't going to get away with their crimes.

Not if he had his way.

Rage exploded through Ronald.

And then he snapped.

✕

WHEN THE SHERIFF SPOTTED RONALD Hammerstein sitting on the lawn in front of his home, the career lawman knew there was some element of truth to the frantic calls his office had received.

Not because of how or where Ronald was sitting, exactly, but because of how far away his neighbors were standing. Normally when something bad went down, you had to fight with the public to maintain the sanctity of the scene. These people were keeping their distance without any encouragement.

The sheriff put his hand on his holster and slowly approached Ronald, who sat motionless in the light of the full moon. There were dark streaks on the music teacher's clothes and face. The air was ripe with a sour mixture of blood and vomit.

"Mr. Hammerstein?"

The teacher gradually raised his head like a man coming out of a dream. Once the fighting and the screaming had ended, he had collapsed from exhaustion. He had sat there, silently, and hadn't moved since, not even when the screaming around him started again. At times the screaming seemed to be everywhere, but he blocked out the noise and he thought about how much he loved his wife and how much he missed her and how he would give anything for her to be alive again.

"Ronald, what happened here?"

"They attacked me with knives." His words were unhurried and his eyes twinkled like diamonds in the moonlight. "They wanted to fight, and I had to, I had to. After what they did, someone had to show them they couldn't be human monsters, not here, not in our town. I guess I had one final lesson for my former students after all."

"Ronald, *what* did you do?"

"They wanted to fight, but they gave me an advantage."

The sheriff glanced at the overturned lawnmower and the two bulky trash bags on the edge of the driveway. He nudged one bag with his shoe. It was full. The mower must have weighed fifty pounds, but the blades were coated in blood, which was dripping and forming sticky puddles on the pavement.

"Ronald, what was your advantage?"

The music teacher grinned, showing his teeth. "I had the bigger blade."

LOVING ROGER

EVERYONE MAKES MISTAKES, A TRUTH Patty knew all too well, which was why she believed in the power of forgiving and forgetting. Her mamma always said forgiveness was love and love was forgiveness. In the end, Patty knew Mamma was right. No matter what mistakes Roger had made, Patty could never stop loving her husband.

The city noise pounded against Patty's temples as she slowed the rental car to a stop at one of the many busy intersections between her and the suburbs. The summer day would have been beautiful if she had been anywhere else in the world. A tractor-trailer roared past, horn blaring, engine snarling, black puffs of smoke spitting out of the chrome pipes behind the cab as the driver ran the red light.

Patty couldn't wait to escape the city. She had felt trapped in the rundown motel where she had been collecting her thoughts, and she would never go back there again. That place was loud and dirty and everyone was rude. The walls were made of cinderblock and the neighbors were so dangerous that all of the windows had metal bars on them.

"Everything will be better," Patty said, focusing on her goals. "I've learned from our mistakes."

She reached for the bottle of cheap champagne on the passenger seat, just to make sure it hadn't shifted. She worried about having the alcohol in the car. She wasn't even sure if that was legal and the new Patty who was driving home again almost didn't care. She and Roger had never imbibed, and she had begun to believe that was a mistake on her part. They needed to loosen up a little.

After confirming the champagne was okay, Patty removed a compact from her brand new purse. The price sticker and bar code were still affixed to the bottom of the peach-colored plastic shell. Her dress was also brand new, as were the lacy red bra and panties and the high-heeled shoes. She had never worn anything like this before. She wondered what her mamma would say and then she pushed the thought away.

Patty flipped the compact open and checked her makeup, lipstick, and hair in the tiny mirror. She felt so much older these days. Lines had formed under her eyes. Their fight had aged her badly, but she thought the makeup hid most of the damage.

Yes, there had been some problems lately, but those problems weren't *all* Roger's fault. Patty was seeing the world differently now. While in the run-down motel, she had found herself with a lot of free time to *really* contemplate what she wanted out of life, and what she had decided she wanted was to fix their mistakes and move forward. She hoped Roger felt the same way. They had to work together if they wanted to get back on the right track.

"Tonight, we'll make up for lost time," Patty said.

The light changed and someone behind her honked.

Patty raised her middle finger to the other driver—another thing she had never done before—and then she headed home, not looking back.

AN HOUR LATER, PATTY SLOWED to a stop in front of the two-story house deep in the heart of the suburbs. The street was tree-lined and the sidewalks were decorated with children's chalk drawings. Lush lawns dotted with trimmed shrubs and beautiful gardens surrounded the well-maintained homes. Everything was more colorful today than Patty ever remembered it being. More beautiful. More alive.

She realized she really *was* seeing life differently. She checked her watch and smiled. Roger wouldn't leave work for at least an hour. The champagne bottle would be chilled by then, and she would be ready to start their relationship anew.

She stepped onto the lawn. The grass was green and soft. A newfound love for her home and her yard and her neighborhood washed over Patty. Her heart fluttered and her skin quivered with unexpected warmth. She never wanted to leave again.

Patty approached the front door and shifted the bottle of champagne under her arm. As she reached for the doorknob, she stopped dead in her tracks.

She had forgotten her house key.

Panic rose inside of Patty and her breathing became clipped. Her hands trembled. She was so close to making things right again and then something like this had to happen. How could she have been so stupid? Her plan was ruined!

"No," Patty whispered. *"No,* I can do this."

She sucked in two deep breaths and then made her way around to the back of the house, pushing through the flowering bushes that enclosed the brick patio. She crossed the patio and stopped at the sliding glass door. She said a little prayer, reached for the handle, and pushed. The door slid open with a squeal.

Patty smiled brightly and stepped into the kitchen, the bottle of champagne gripped tightly in her hand. The yellow patterned linoleum floor was spotless and the ceiling fan spun in lazy circles. Cool air washed over her sweaty skin.

Something was different, though. On the counter was a wooden knife block holding seven specialty knives. Patty had always wanted a set like that, had pointed them out to Roger a million times at Monkey Ward, but he always claimed they were too expensive. Then she noticed an even more dramatic change: the new Kenmore refrigerator. She hardly believed her eyes. She had wanted a new refrigerator since they first moved into the house so many years ago and Roger always said they couldn't afford one.

Excitement rose inside of Patty and her heartbeat quickened. Had Roger come to the same realization she had during their separation? Was he making an effort to win her back, too? What else might he have planned? Her mind spun at the possibilities.

Yet, something wasn't right and her heart understood that before her brain. A frown formed on Patty's tired face.

There were comic strips and newspaper clippings and "honey do" lists held to the refrigerator by a variety of magnets. Some of the magnets were shaped like animals, others like clouds, and still others like fruits and vegetables.

None of these magnets or the collected pieces of paper belonged to Patty.

"Who are you?" a woman asked from the dining room. "What are you doing?"

Patty spun around and the champagne bottle slammed into the edge of the kitchen counter. Patty and the other woman both jumped in surprise as the bottle shattered. The liquid inside sprayed into the air as shards of glass skipped across the floor on a wave of foamy liquid.

A moment passed and neither woman moved. Then their eyes rose from the wet mess and locked on each other.

"Who are you?" the woman asked again. She laughed nervously. She was much younger than Patty, with blonde hair and blue eyes and trim legs. The woman reminded Patty of the girls she had known in her college days, back when she first met Roger at a mixer. Patty had seen how Roger looked at those girls.

"*Who* are *you*?" Patty asked. A knot twisted in her stomach.

"My name is Sally." The woman's voice was a little less harsh this time, showing a hint of concern. "Are you okay, hon? What are you doing here?"

"I live here with Roger. What are *you* doing here?"

"I'm sorry. You must be confused," the woman said. "This is my house."

Patty finally realized who this woman was, who this woman had to be. The whore. This was the god-damned whore who had seduced her husband!

The rage Patty had been suppressing for a lifetime boiled over. Waves of heat flowed through her body and her hands trembled from the surge of adrenaline. A lot of people had taken advantage of Patty over the years, but she had never been so consumed by anger when faced with their betrayals.

Patty's vision flashed red as she reached for the wooden block on the counter and selected the largest knife. When she turned back toward the dining room, she saw the shock on the whore's face.

Patty took a step, kicking the base of the broken champagne bottle across the foamy kitchen floor.

"No, wait a minute," the woman said as she backed away, raising her hands. "What are you doing?"

As Patty moved, she remembered the events of a day much like this one many years ago when she had come home early from work.

She had discovered Roger and that woman from across the street doing terrible things like animals in heat. God, the awful sounds they had made!

Patty's anger and confusion merged with the memory of the endless river of blood splattering everywhere. Patty was home again and she saw every little detail and she had to do *something* to make them stop.

The woman named Sally, now backed into a corner, said: "Please don't hurt me! Please listen!"

But Patty couldn't listen. She had to make Roger and the awful woman stop what they were doing. She had to help Roger understand the mistake he was making.

She loved him so goddamned much. Why couldn't he understand that?

Patty raised the knife and prepared to show her husband exactly how much she loved him, and she would keep showing him until he understood that her love was endless and eternal.

She would love Roger again and again, and she would never, ever stop.

AMONG US

I'VE LEARNED A LOT LATELY about the terrible things you can do *if* you're motivated enough.

Six months ago I was a good, upstanding citizen with a beautiful wife and two amazing children and a great job doing what I loved: standing up for the little guy.

Yes, I was a lawyer, but don't hold that against me. I was the good kind of lawyer, and please don't make any jokes about the good kind being the dead kind. I'm in no mood for jokes these days.

My love for my wife and kids was endless, even though I spent most of my waking hours at work. Like most people, I worked hard because I wanted the best for my family, which was a good deal for the law firm of Jacobs, Michener, and Johnson since my desire and drive made me one of their most loyal and productive employees. Once I set my sights on a goal, I burned the candle at both ends until the job was finished.

So when I arrived at work after the Fourth of July weekend last year and found a message saying I needed to be at an emergency meeting of the Partners, I thought all of my hard work was paying off.

You see, I had recently discovered information that helped us grab a car manufacturer by the ball-bearings: some rather incriminating safety reports they had "misfiled" in one of their subsidiary offices in the middle of nowhere. When the evidence was brought to their attention, they settled out of court and our law firm took our standard 40% of the $1.1 billion settlement.

The message said the meeting was starting in just a few minutes, so I dropped everything and hurried to the ninth floor. I took a deep breath as I exited the elevator and crossed a lobby with marble floors and vaulted ceilings. The opulence was stunning, humbling, and inspiring all at the same time.

An executive assistant was sitting at her desk outside the main conference room, wearing a phone headset and typing away on her computer. Her name was Alice and she handled all of the scheduling for the big bosses. No one saw them or spoke to them without her putting it on the calendar first. She was the gatekeeper to three of the most powerful men in the city, which made *her* pretty darn powerful, too.

Alice glanced up, smiled, and said: "Go right on in, Mr. Smith. The Partners are expecting you."

Just hearing those words made my heart skip a beat.

I pushed the tall wooden door open and entered the conference room paid for with billions of dollars of judgments over the years. It truly was a breathtaking sight.

Chandeliers crisscrossed the ornate ceiling and sparkling rays of sunlight radiated in through the massive windows overlooking the river. The walls were lined with handcrafted bookcases, each twenty feet tall. The shelves held copies of every legal text since the beginning of the written law.

In the middle of the room was a polished table surrounded by plush chairs on the wide oriental carpet. Seven men were already sitting there, but the Partners were nowhere to be seen. These seven men were senior lawyers I recognized from around the building, although I hadn't worked closely with any of them.

A moment after I sat down, one of the bookcases opened into the room, revealing it was actually a hidden door to the Partners' private offices.

Peter Jacobs, Robert Michener, and Thomas Johnson emerged from the doorway and everyone at the table stood. The Partners were in their early fifties with matching suits, distinguished salt and pepper hair, and handcrafted Swiss wristwatches. Their *shoes* cost what I made in a year.

Someone started to clap and then the rest of us joined in, which was as surreal as it sounds. The clapping echoed around the immense chamber. I guess it was just a nervous reaction. Like I said before, these were three of the most powerful men in the city and they could get into any meeting with anyone, but only the chosen few got to meet with them. They had mansions in the most elite neighborhoods, fabulous trophy wives, and stunningly successful children. They were the living, breathing American dream. Hell, Robert Michener owned his own (albeit small) Caribbean island.

I hadn't spoken with the Partners once during my entire time at the firm and I had certainly never been called to a meeting like this.

Maybe no one had. Something was up. Something *big*.

Robert Michener waved his hand to get us to stop and sit back down, smiling his bright white smile. The Partners took their places at the end of the table in their ornate, oversized chairs. The rest of us returned to our seats.

Peter Jacobs said: "Gentlemen, we have to be certain this meeting stays strictly confidential. Please put your cell phones, PDAs, and keys on the table."

The eight of us did as we were told without any objection.

Jacobs continued: "I'm sorry to rush you up here on such short notice, but we have important issues to discuss. We're taking all of you on as new Partners."

I was speechless. You're taught to have a face of stone in the courtroom—it should appear as if everything's going just as you expected, no matter what happens, even if your client just accidentally confessed—but this wasn't merely a surprise piece of testimony or a slip of the tongue on the witness stand.

This was *huge*. There were eight of us... *eight* new Partners!

My first thought was simple disbelief. Yes, I had worked my butt off for years, but becoming a Partner? Now? Where was the hidden camera, right?

My second thought was so hopeful and full of joy it pains me to write this: I couldn't wait to call Melinda to tell her the news.

This offer was what we had been dreaming about for so long. It would make up for the long hours I had spent in this building and out on the road working cases. It would justify all of the important moments I had already missed: Alan's first steps, Christy's birth, and almost every other significant landmark in my children's lives to date.

Jacobs continued: "There's been a major change at the firm and we need your help. We've joined with a much larger group."

This was almost a bigger shock than the news that there would be eight new Partners. Jacobs, Michener, and Johnson had merged with another law firm? How could that have happened without anyone knowing? Office rumors bounce around like ricocheting bullets, but nothing like a merger had *ever* been mentioned at the water cooler or via a gossipy e-mail.

Michener said: "It's a much larger cause. One we believe in wholeheartedly. You men are here to represent your departments, to help make the change easier for everyone. But first, you need to join us. You must join us and become Partners!"

He bellowed this last sentence almost theatrically and something in his voice didn't sound quite right. A sense of unease suddenly nagged at me deep in my gut.

"Join us," Johnson said, standing and removing his jacket. He began unbuttoning his shirt, slowly from the top. I sat there stunned. Now this was *really* too surreal. Was I dreaming? Was there a punchline to come? Men like the Partners aren't exactly known for their sense of humor, and the whispering voice of doubt in the back of my mind grew louder.

When Johnson reached the last button, the entire room lit up with blue lightning. When the flash faded, sunspots floated in my field of vision.

I stood and backed away. The Partners were staring at me, their eyes widening and their mouths dropping open. They were shocked and I quickly realized why. The seven other lawyers who had come for this meeting were sitting motionless, their unblinking eyes locked on Johnson. They looked like zombies... or maybe corpses.

"He's one of *them*," Jacobs stated coldly. "Take care of the rest, Johnson, and I'll deal with this troublemaker."

Johnson finished removing his shirt. He stood there, proudly displaying his pale white skin and graying hair and slightly rolling stomach.

Then something happened.

His abdomen twitched, the muscles twisting through his flesh, forming some kind of horrible face on his round belly. Two ruby-colored eyes popped open below his nipples and a jagged horizontal line ripped across the bottom of his abdomen, revealing a rotting mouth filled with green slime.

The mouth yawned, as if just waking up.

I screamed and backed away, knocking my chair over. I yelled at my colleagues, trying to compel them to move, but it was too late. Their chests were expanding through their shirts, bubbling and mutating like vats of chemicals in some old science fiction movie.

Jacobs reached for me and I did the only thing I could: I kicked him in the groin, sending him to the floor like a sack of bricks. His face turned bright red and a slight cry escaped from between his lips.

I never was much of a fighter, so I make no apologies for my methods.

I ran for the door, turning the doorknob and throwing myself against the door, expecting it to be locked.

It wasn't.

The door flew open and banged against the lobby wall. I stumbled and tripped, sliding across the polished marble floor. The world seemed off its axis as I hobbled toward the stairs while Alice the executive assistant watched in amazement. Her wide eyes suggested either she had no idea what was happening in the conference room or she hadn't expected someone to escape.

I hurried down the stairs, only slowing when I finally realized no one was chasing me. Why would they bother? Security would most likely be waiting for me in the lobby, after all. That was the quick and easy way to end the situation before it could escalate.

Instead of continuing any further, I exited at the third floor and navigated my way through the rows of cubicles where dozens of clerks worked on cases. Real offices with doors encircled the cube world. One of them was mine, but I never stopped.

My destination was the back stairs to the basement, which was home to the boilers and other mechanicals necessary for a building that size. There were also vast rooms of filing cabinets containing tens of thousands of folders from old cases.

If I needed somewhere to hide, that was a good place, but deep down I knew I had to leave the building fast. Hiding just meant the Partners would find me sooner or later, and I didn't want to learn what they did to "troublemakers."

I reached for my cell phone, not quite sure what to tell 911 and then my wife ("hey, my bosses are monsters and they're recruiting!"), but my pocket was empty. My phone and keys were still sitting on the table in the conference room.

"Fuck," I muttered, hurrying down the stairs.

I ignored the door to the lobby and kept moving, listening for any sound that might indicate my pursuers were closing in.

At the bottom of the stairwell I pushed open the heavy metal fire door and made my way through the maze of storage areas and mechanical rooms until I found the dock door in the rear of the building's basement.

I took a deep breath, reached down, and tugged on the metal handle. The door rumbled along its metal tracks. The intense sunlight pouring in was nearly blinding after being in the dimly lit basement.

Part of me expected security guards or maybe even the Partners themselves to be waiting on the other side, but there was no one in the loading area.

Without keys, my car was useless, so I stuck to the side streets and searched for a payphone to call Melinda and warn her to not answer the door until I got home, but there wasn't a phone booth to be found anywhere. Apparently the city had been getting rid of them for some time since the spread of cell phones really took off. I was too busy working to notice, I guess.

I flagged down a cab and gave the driver my home address. When I asked to use his cell phone, he gestured that he didn't understand me, but that might have been a lie. I must have looked like a crazy man, even in my expensive suit, because the driver kept glancing at me in the mirror while he drove.

My mind spun during the trip from the city to the suburbs. There were so many questions. What the hell had happened to the Partners? When did it happen? What exactly were they? What did they want?

The events of those five minutes in the conference room were too impossible and absurd to truly comprehend, yet I never doubted my sanity for an instant. I was too scared to be insane and my hands were shaking badly by the time the cab stopped in the driveway of my two-story colonial in the picturesque neighborhood my family called home. No real mansions here, but a lot of McMansions for sure.

I paid the driver, jumped out, and ran to the front door, which was unlocked and slightly open. A lump formed in my throat. There was no good reason for the door to be open. None at all. We *never* left that door open.

I stepped inside the foyer. I heard voices upstairs and then Melinda appeared in the doorway of the guest bedroom.

She saw me and asked: "What's wrong? Is it the kids?"

Before I could answer, a cell phone rang in the room behind my wife. She glanced over her shoulder. A voice answered the cell quietly, but I heard him well enough.

I said: "Who's up there?"

A look of confusion crossed Melinda's face as two hands appeared out of nowhere to jerk her back into the bedroom. The door slammed shut.

I dashed up the steps two at a time and kicked at the door, which popped open without any resistance. The privacy locks on modern doors are pretty much useless, just FYI.

On the far side of the room, one of the new Partners held Melinda. His shirt was open and the red eyes below his chest were pulsating. The muscles that formed the monster's mouth were moving and leaking green slime.

"Get him," the monster growled to its host.

The Partner left Melinda where she stood and approached me.

Instead of falling back on the classic kick to the groin, I threw the best punch I could. My fist landed directly on his chin, but he didn't flinch. My knuckles, though, felt like someone had smacked them with a hammer.

The Partner smiled and returned the favor, slugging me in the gut. The pain radiated throughout my entire body. I fell backwards into the dresser and gasped for air.

The Partner motioned at me in a way that said "come here and try it again," so I did. What other choice did I have?

With my stomach and hand still roaring in pain, I inched toward the Partner, sucking in deep breaths.

When I was within striking distance, I punched him in the chest as hard as I could, my fist landing true on the monster's face.

This time the Partner stumbled backwards, the agony obvious in his bulging eyes. The monster in his chest looked livid. I grabbed Melinda and backed us out of the room.

"He's... he's..." she started to babble.

"Yes, he's one of *them*," I said, pulling her with me to our master bedroom. I slammed the door shut and opened the closet. My father's old service revolver was hidden in a shoebox on the top shelf.

"We have to get Alan and Christy and get out of town," I said, quickly loading the gun. Melinda didn't answer.

I turned. The bedroom door was open and the new Partner stood next to my wife.

"I don't understand why you're like this, but let us try to change you," Melinda said. "We can at least try. The change makes everything better."

My heart sunk and I felt like someone was punching me in the stomach all over again. My wife was one of *them,* but I couldn't believe it. Didn't want to believe it. Didn't have the capacity in my heart or head to consider the idea.

"Get him, you fool," the monster growled from the Partner's belly.

He moved in my direction. I had never fired the gun in my life, but this wasn't a human being coming toward me. This was a monster that couldn't be reasoned with.

My shaking hand raised the gun and pulled the trigger. The gunshot was louder than I expected and I screamed as the right side of the Partner's head ripped open... but he didn't die. He actually laughed.

The Partner kept coming for me, half of his brains leaking onto his shoulder. He staggered from side to side like he was drunk. I pulled the trigger twice more. The first bullet hit his open mouth, blowing out two of his teeth and sending blood flying everywhere, stopping his laughter, but still not killing him.

The second bullet, though, found the sweet spot, hitting one of the *monster's* glowing eyes, which exploded in a splash of bloody slime. The monster screamed in pain as the Partner dropped to a knee. Green brain matter poured out of the wound.

I stepped forward and put the gun's barrel directly against the monster's other eye, which widened in terror. The Partner reached for me as I pulled the trigger. The gunshot was loud and abrupt, and the Partner fell backwards against the wall and slumped to the floor.

His chest was a catastrophe of blood and pus and tangled muscles, and his flesh pulsated the same color as the eyes had a moment before. Then there was a flash of blue lightning and the monster's face healed over. The eyes and the mouth vanished, all in a matter of seconds, as if they had never been there in the first place.

Now the man was just a dead lawyer in my master bedroom. That certainly couldn't end well.

I looked at my wife. She had unbuttoned her blouse and she wasn't wearing a bra. The muscles below her breasts began to twitch as she slipped the blouse off.

The monster was emerging from within her beautiful flesh and there was a coldness behind her eyes, a darkness lurking within the woman I knew better than anyone else in the world. It was the monster. A monster inside the woman I loved.

She charged.

✕

A FEW MINUTES LATER THE front door of the house swung open.

I was sobbing in my hands when Alan appeared in the doorway to the master bedroom. My five-year-old boy was carrying baby Christy in his arms. His expression was cold and collected. Her face displayed a chilly smile I had never seen before.

They had both been changed.

Now that I knew what to look for, that coldness behind their eyes, I could see the monster inside of them even if they looked normal otherwise. My heart broke again.

"Come join us, Daddy," my son said. "Pretty please? I'll be the best little boy ever if you do. Let us try to change you again. The change feels wonderful."

Sitting there next to my wife's dead body, my wife who no longer showed any sign of the monster that had dwelled within her, I couldn't think of anything I wanted more than to be with my family one more time, to be a real family, to just be together with no worries in the world.

But that wasn't possible.

I had to make a choice: stay and be killed by the monsters when they couldn't change me into one of their own, or go on surviving and try to learn to live with what I had done.

In the end, I made the choice I had to make.

I leapt to my feet and pushed past my son and daughter, throwing myself into the Partner who was waiting for me at the bottom of the stairs, sending him flying across the foyer. My shoulder hurt from the impact. It was like I had run into a brick wall. This was more rough-and-tumble physical activity than I had experienced since my ill-advised attempt to join the football team in seventh grade.

I dashed through the kitchen, grabbed a set of car keys off the hook in the mudroom, and hurried into the garage. As I jumped into my wife's BMW, I heard my son yelling at the Partner in the foyer. He sounded so adult, so *pissed*.

I started the car, shifted into reverse, and floored the gas, crashing back through the garage door. I turned onto the street and floored the gas again as I sped past the black SUV parked at the curb.

I raced for the highway.

I never returned.

✕

A FEW HOURS LATER, I called my house from an old-fashioned phone booth outside a biker bar. Not everyone in the boonies had a cell phone yet, it seemed. Or maybe no one from the phone company could be bothered to drive so far into the middle of nowhere to disassemble it.

I don't know why I called, but I did.

My son answered. He said something in his way-too-adult voice that I haven't forgotten. The words still ring in my mind every morning when I awaken from the nightmares.

He said: "Don't worry, we'll find you, Daddy, and we're not going to change you, we're going to kill you. Wherever you go, one of us will be there... soon... very soon... we're everywhere."

I hung up and cried in the phone booth, holding my head and mourning the loss of my wife and son and daughter. In my mind, they were all dead. That was the only way to keep my sanity, which I thought I was on the verge of losing anyway.

When the tears finally stopped, I made a plan. Planning was what got me through the long years of college and the long days and nights of climbing the ladder at the law firm. Planning for a better future was what had allowed me to dedicate so much of myself to my work.

The first thing I needed to do would have been easier twenty years ago, but it wasn't impossible.

I had to disappear and drop off the radar. Who knew what access the Partners might have to the government and law enforcement? They *could* find me if they wanted to, I was sure of that, and I was also sure they weren't just going to accept that I was immune to their powers and let me go on my merry way.

That night, I maxed out the available cash advances on my credit cards and emptied my checking account before tossing my wallet in a public trash can.

The next day, in some no stoplight town that time forgot, I ditched my wife's BMW behind an abandoned house and bought a beaten Ford Bronco from a slimy used car salesman with a gold tooth who didn't seem to care that I had no identification since I was paying cash.

Soon I was traveling the country, stocking up on weapons through private sales. I did everything I could to get better at fighting and hunting and living off the grid.

You see, I'm not only a hard worker, but a fast learner.

These days I can move from place to place without attracting attention, set traps and ambushes like someone born in a war-torn country, and I can hit a moving target at a surprisingly long distance.

I'm not the person I used to be, but I am the person I had to become.

✕

I HAVE TO SIGN OFF now, but if you haven't been changed, get away from the cities.

Wherever there are people, there is danger.

Among Us

I have no way of guessing how many of them exist, but they're growing in number every day.

I'm dealing with the ones I can safely dispatch, but it's tough to keep a low profile while you're destroying monsters, so I've had to let many pass by. You can't just shoot a monster twice in the chest in the middle of a diner without compromising yourself. You have to follow him and watch for a good opportunity, which doesn't always present itself.

But if you're reading this, get yourself to safety and be careful. These monsters look like you and me and they won't stop until they have us all.

Maybe it's too late, but maybe not.

Like I said earlier, I've always dedicated myself to my work, even if it meant sacrificing other things I loved.

My work now is simple: to hunt the Partners until they're all dead.

I'll learn everything I can and soon *they* won't know what hit them.

Just remember... *they're among us.*

NOT WITHOUT REGRETS

WHEN SARAH WAS A LITTLE girl, her grandmother gave her a piece of advice that resonated with her so strongly she never forgot it: make every day count and live without regrets because no one gets out alive.

Those words were spoken in her grandmother's apartment in a retirement community the cheerful old woman called God's Waiting Room, and two decades later Sarah could recall the conversation with an oddly perfect clarity.

Sarah had taken the advice to heart, but that certainly didn't mean she claimed to have no regrets about her life to date. How could she when her ex-husband was currently living in a padded room in a state hospital? Their lives would never be the same after what he had done to her and their little girl. Emma still loved her father more than anything, probably because she was too young to remember the horror of what happened three years ago. Sarah remembered well enough for both of them, though, and those memories provided her with more than her fair share of regrets.

A fierce thunderstorm was rolling across the valley, but Sarah didn't mind. Nothing much scared her these days, not after what she had been through. The television was turned to the eleven o'clock news, but the sound was muted and she wasn't actually watching. Instead she was debating whether to check on Emma again. Most of Sarah's nights were sleepless and she couldn't help but look in on her daughter again and again, even though the compulsion was bordering on unhealthy.

She sat on the couch in the living room, one hand caressing the ornate wooden cane resting on her lap. Sharp pains still ripped through her whenever she put all of her weight on her right leg, so the cane was a godsend. And although her leg was disfigured, her upper body was stronger than ever. When she was honest with herself, she was surprised by how powerful her arms had become. She didn't discuss with anyone why she spent so much time in the gym. No one else would understand she was preparing for the day when David would be free to come after them again.

Lightning split the night and thunder rumbled, shaking the house. The power flickered, but not enough to turn off the television, and when Sarah glanced at the newscast, she saw something that nearly took her breath away.

The words BREAKING NEWS: RIOT AT MENTAL HEALTH FACILITY were superimposed over a file photo of the state hospital located on the outskirts of town, the place where David had spent the last three years ranting and raving at the doctors.

Sarah grabbed the remote and fumbled with the buttons until the television blared: "...sources within the hospital report at least three people are dead and dozens have been injured. State Police on the scene are not releasing the names of the victims. Several patients have reportedly escaped the facility and could be somewhere on the grounds or in the woods nearby. The State Police are setting up roadblocks..."

Sarah turned the television off. There was no need to hear more. She clutched her cane and staggered to her feet. She wanted to believe this was just another nightmare, but then her knee smacked the corner of the coffee table and the sharp stab of pain told her she was awake.

She hurried to the front door, her mind spinning with panic, her cane thumping the floor like a hammer. She didn't bother with the light switch as she entered the foyer. She could see what she needed well enough in the glow of the nightlight at the top of the stairs. Both the deadbolt and the regular lock were secured. There was no reason for them not to be, but still, she was relieved to see the locks undisturbed. She peered out one of the narrow windows next to the door. The lawn was drowning in pools of water and the world was a dark curtain beyond her home.

You've gotta stay calm, she thought, glancing up the stairs at Emma's bedroom door. She desperately wanted to check on her little girl, but first she had to take care of one more thing if she were to have any peace of mind.

Sarah hobbled to the kitchen, her bad leg screaming at her as she went. She hadn't stretched properly, she hadn't moved in a thoughtful manner, she hadn't obeyed any of the rules for protecting her leg from injury—and it was letting her know there would be hell to pay.

When Sarah reached the kitchen, she checked the back door. Both of those locks were secured, too. Again she felt a sense of relief. She backed into the middle of the kitchen, leaned on her cane, and took several deep breaths.

Gotta stay calm, she thought. *Gotta think clearly. Be cool, be calm, and think.*

The words soothed her, brought her down to a more relaxed state, but then a quick movement in the darkness of the backyard caught her eye. She approached the window above the sink, leaning closer to the glass for a better view. At first she couldn't see anything beyond the torrential downpour, not even the woods. Rain and darkness had swallowed the entire world.

Then lightning split the sky and the backyard lit up, making her jump in surprise.

In the brief moment of blinding clarity, Sarah saw Emma's tire swing spinning wildly and tree branches bending in the savage wind. The rain beat against the window with a marching band's cadence.

But there was no one there.

She caught her breath and laughed. She had been certain David would be standing in the middle of the yard, closing in on the house like a horror movie villain.

She wondered if she looked as silly as she suddenly felt. The state hospital was miles away and the weather was awful. Had David somehow managed to escape, which was impossible considering he was on the most secure floor of the entire building, there were road-blocks and cops on patrol and endless ways for him to be stopped long before he reached the house.

Sarah laughed again, putting her hand over her face and rubbing her eyes. She needed to get some sleep. That was the real problem. How long had it been since she got a decent night's rest? Three years? And how many times did she peek into Emma's bedroom each and every night? Dozens? Hundreds?

Then Sarah heard a window shatter in the basement and in that instant she knew all of her worst fears were coming true after all.

Shit, shit, shit, he's here, she thought, the panic consuming her. *I have to protect Emma!*

Lightning flashed and thunder exploded almost instantaneously. They were in the heart of the storm. The power died. No flickering lights. No drama. No warning.

In the dark, Sarah opened one of the high kitchen cabinets and swatted around until she found a small cardboard box she had stashed there many years ago when romantic dinners had still been part of her life. She carefully lowered the box, but it slipped out of her hands and landed on the floor with a loud thud.

She dropped to her knees, sending a howl of pain from her bad leg throughout her body. She groped blindly until she found the thin candle in a metal base and a few loose matches. She struggled to her feet, leaned against the counter, and struck a match. The tip flared to life, releasing the harsh odor of sulfur dioxide. She lit the candle. The yellow glow of the burning wick filled the room with dancing light.

Sarah retrieved her sharpest carving knife from the drawer next to the stove before making her way to the basement door. She paused there, considering her options. Her heart was racing, she could barely think, and she had to do *something,* but what?

She had envisioned so many different scenarios for David's return, but this wasn't one of them, and now that the moment was here, all of the thousands of hours lifting weights and working out didn't feel like nearly enough preparation. Why hadn't she bought a gun? Why hadn't she and Emma changed their names and moved to some other country?

Sarah shook her head. All of that hindsight was academic and it wasn't helping her think clearly. What mattered now, what was she going to do?

Before she could decide, the basement door swung open toward her, the hinges squealing.

David stood on the top step, nude. He was concentration camp skinny and dripping wet from the rain. His pale, gaunt flesh glistened as lightning illuminated the room and thunder rocked the house again. Streaks of mud covered his legs. Cuts and bruises from his escape marked his flesh.

"Oh shit," Sarah muttered, her eyes widening in horror.

David grinned, grabbed his wife by the shirt, and pulled her forward. Gravity took over from there, sending her tumbling down the steps.

Pinpricks of light erupted inside her eyelids with each blow to her head on the way down, and then she felt nothing.

✕

When Sarah awoke, she wanted to believe David's return had been just another bad dream, but the excruciating pain was all too real. Every bone, every muscle, every nerve in her body shrieked.

She forced her groggy eyes open. The basement

was almost completely dark, the only light being from the candle she had dropped at the top of the steps and the occasional flash of lightning outside the high, narrow windows. The storm had moved further east, so time had definitely passed.

Sarah turned her head and winced as a sharp pain tore through her neck, but she resisted the urge to scream. She was curled in a fetal position on the concrete floor at the bottom of the steps. Blood trickled from a wound in her forehead.

She realized she was naked. David must have stripped her while she was unconscious, but how long had she been here? And where was he now? If something happened to her daughter, she didn't think she could go on living with the guilt.

"You awake, Sarah?"

David emerged from a darkened corner where he had been watching her. He was still naked. He circled her with his hands hidden behind his back.

"Please, David, don't do this."

"Sarah, Sarah, Sarah," he said, dragging out her name long and slow. "Do you have any regrets about what you've done?"

"David, you don't want to do…"

"No, Sarah, no! I *do* want to do this! I need answers, goddammit."

"What kind of answers?"

"For one, do you regret putting me in that place?"

"David," Sarah replied cautiously, "You tried to kill me and Em. I couldn't let you hurt our daughter. You were out of control. You needed help. You *need* help."

"Fuck you, Sarah. You're the one who needs help."

David brought his hands out into the open and Sarah's carving knife gleamed in the candlelight. He knelt and lowered the blade to her throat. The knife's tip pushed into her flesh, just a little, but he didn't go for the kill. Not yet.

"Sarah, I don't think I can forgive you, do you understand that? At least not until you explain why you betrayed me."

"You know what, David?" Sarah said, a righteous rage suddenly welling within her. "*Fuck you.* How's that for an explanation? Fuck you for what you did."

David backhanded her across the face, sending

a wave of stars through her field of vision. Her head rolled loosely on her neck, which roared in pain.

"Fuck *you*, Sarah, how do you like *that*," David said, slamming her head sideways into the concrete floor.

Her lungs ached and she coughed, a ribbon of blood spitting out between her lips. With her head turned and blood pouring out of her mouth, she spotted something that seized her attention. She had to force herself to look back up at David, so he wouldn't know what she had seen.

"Don't hurt yourself," David whispered. "That's my job. I'm here to make you pay for what you did."

Sarah knew she had to buy herself some time to make her move. She sucked in a painful breath and asked: "Why are you *really* doing this?"

David's eyes widened and his face twisted with rage.

"Sarah, you dumb bitch, you blamed me after you killed Em and those goddamned police *believed* you! You ruined our lives, you ruined *everything,* and now you're going to pay for it!"

Sarah hadn't realized how bad her husband's delusions had become, but she didn't have time to think about that. While he ranted, her right hand blindly reached for her cane, which had snapped in half during the fall, landing just a few feet away. Her fingertips found the rounded grip and she grabbed on tight.

Lightning flashed, illuminating David's nude and blood-spattered body poised over her like a native preparing a ritual sacrifice. His eyes were bright and wild. His mouth was expelling insane thoughts that made no sense. His ribs showed through his pale flesh. He began to bring the knife down in an arc toward her chest.

Time slowed as Sarah pulled her arm back as far as she could, using the same motion she practiced when thumping the heavy bag at the gym. When her elbow smacked the concrete floor, she drove the broken cane forward with all her might.

David's ranting ended in a deep sucking sound as the jagged end of the cane slammed into his abdomen. As his hands reflexively came together in front of his body, the knife flew off to the right and skidded across the floor. A sickening yelp escaped his throat as his flesh ripped open. Sarah screamed and twisted as hard as she could.

David stared into Sarah's blazing eyes as if he couldn't figure out what had suddenly happened. Then he tipped backwards, the cane sticking out of his belly like an arrow, his hands still clutching it. His head hit the floor with a loud crack.

And then there was silence, except for the rain and the thunder.

Sarah stared in horror at her husband. She couldn't look away. She had to make sure he was really dead.

She also couldn't stop hearing David say that she had *killed* their daughter. That was ludicrous. He had truly gone insane.

Yet she carefully circled around the statement again and again, as if it were a dangerous animal.

She watched David's cooling corpse and she couldn't quite bring herself to ask the questions forming in her aching head... like why hadn't Emma been woken by the storm, and when was the last time she had actually seen her daughter, and what would she find when she went upstairs to check the cute little pink bedroom next to her own.

Sometime later, Sarah got her answers.

WHAT THEY
LEFT BEHIND

SCOTT SODERMAN STOOD IN THE open dock
door as rain pounded the warehouse's parking lot
and the forest beyond. To his right were the rented
trailers waiting at the other doors to be emptied.
Below him was a storm drain clogged with leaves,
debris, and trash that had collected during the years
the Timlico complex sat abandoned. Dirty water
pooled like a lake.

By the entrance to the parking lot, nearly lost in
the overgrown grasses, was an enormous and faded
sign: *Office/Warehouse/Flex Space For Sale/Lease.* The
realtor had nailed a hopeful and bright *LEASED!*

banner across the front just yesterday. Scott suspected she was probably the talk of the local real estate community for finally landing a tenant for this place.

The Timlico Logistics Corporation had built the warehouse and the attached offices as their east coast operations center in the 1970s. It was state of the art at the time, but the property had been deteriorating for years, sitting unoccupied since the sudden closure of the company a decade before. The remnants of the offices next door were rotting within the vine-covered walls and roof. The warehouse was still solid, though. Steel, concrete, and sheet metal endured the ravages of time better than drywall and carpet, although nothing man-made could last forever. Eventually, Mother Nature would have reclaimed all of this land.

"What a way to spend a Saturday," Scott muttered.

A voice behind him replied: "Yeah, the storm's getting worse."

Scott spun around as George stepped onto the loading dock.

"Jesus Christ man, don't sneak up on me!" Scott dramatically clutched at his chest like he was an old man instead of just shy of turning twenty. "If you kill me, I'm pretty sure my sister will have to dump you and my dad will probably fire your ass and send you back to New Jersey."

George laughed. "Sorry 'bout that. Thought you heard me coming."

"Christ, now I need a smoke. You got a light?" Scott pulled a pack of cigarettes from his pocket. His lighter was in the car and he felt no desire to brave the elements to retrieve it.

"Nada. Those things will kill you before you're fifty."

"If I live that long." Scott returned the pack of cigarettes to his pocket for later. "They calm my nerves."

"If you say so."

"I do. Anyway, there's not much I can actually do here, so I may as well get busy getting cancer."

"Why'd you agree to help then?"

"I would have been dragged along one way or another, but I figured my old man might go easier on me if I volunteered first."

George laughed. "Maybe, maybe not. He's been in rough shape since we lost his biggest client. I just wish we'd had two more weeks to prep for this move. We're trying to get too much done this weekend, which means I'll have to spend the next month fixing our mistakes *and* doing my regular job."

"I guess there wasn't much choice. Dad's getting evicted from the old building on Monday, right?"

"Correctamundo."

"So you guys leased this place on the cheap, but as part of the deal you have to demolish that office building next door?"

"Yep, we agreed to tear it down within the next six months since it'll never be up to code again and our rent was reduced to compensate us for that work. Why?"

"Don't tell anyone, but I want to go find something in there before you get started. A souvenir or whatever, something they left behind. It'll be cool."

"If you say so, Scott. You're a weird guy sometimes."

Mary sped by on the forklift, sounding the horn as she passed, although they heard her coming a mile away. She was busy unloading pallets and crates from the trailers lined up at the dock doors. Scott and George shared a single responsibility that could have been handled by one reasonably competent person: checking the incoming inventory numbers against a master list to ensure each delivery was recorded properly. It was *almost* as if Scott's father didn't trust either one of them not to fuck up the most basic task.

Every hour or so a truck driver brought another fully loaded trailer from the old warehouse where Scott's father and the rest of the employees were busy closing down operations. While Mary unloaded that trailer, the driver returned one of the empty trailers to the other side of town and the process repeated itself. There was a lot to move and it would have been a hectic day even without the bad weather.

Mary stopped the forklift near where Scott and George stood watching the rain. The yellow machine's weary engine growled. The stink of oil and grease emanated from under the hood.

Mary shouted: "Dad called! He says the power keeps cutting out at the old warehouse and we need to check the generator here to figure out if it actually works!"

"Okay, I'll go!" Scott said.

Mary tossed her brother a flashlight. "Take that and watch yourself! You don't want to fall through the floor! George, why don't you go with him and make sure he gets back in one piece?"

Without waiting for an answer—the question had been rhetorical anyway—Mary gunned the fork-lift's engine and rolled into a trailer to grab the next pallet, leaving a cloud of black smoke hanging in her wake. There was no time for chitchat.

George and Scott made their way across the warehouse to the double doors that served as a gateway to the offices. Tacked onto the wall next to the doors was a map of the complex. At first glance the lines on the dusty, oversized paper resembled a giant maze, but the color-code system helped bring some order to the chaos.

"According to the realtor, the generator should be in the basement under the offices," George said. "None of us went down there, though. Hell, we didn't go into the offices. She said it was too dangerous."

"Looks like the stairs to the basement are on the other side of the building," Scott replied, pointing at a square labeled MECHANICAL ROOM #7/ BASEMENT ACCESS. "It's a straight shot, though."

"Okay, let's go. I don't want to spend too long in there."

"Scared of the dark?"

"Don't ask."

"Too late."

They opened the double doors and stared into the pitch-black void while Scott swatted around the wall, finding damp drywall and a series of switches. He flipped them. Some of the lights flickered to life, but not many.

"Holy crap," Scott whispered.

The hallway was eerily cloaked in shadows, but he could see the mess well enough: piles of discarded paperwork, water-stained ceiling tiles that were crumbling and falling onto the carpet, and colorful graffiti on the walls. The trapped stench of mold, mildew, and standing water seeped into the warehouse.

"Watch your step," George said.

Scott used the flashlight to guide them through the wide gaps of gloom where the overhead lights were broken or burned out, but he stopped at the first office with an open door.

A high-backed chair was overturned behind the metal desk, a framed aerial photograph of the property was smashed on the floor, and two filing cabinets were stripped of their drawers. Paperwork, discarded beer cans, used condoms, and crumpled fast-food bags littered the office. Water dripped from a blackened ceiling tile in the corner.

They started walking again. Dozens of offices, conference rooms, and several hallways branched off to their left and right. If there had been any twists and turns along the way to their destination, they surely would have gotten lost for hours. Everything looked the same after a while.

"Why'd they leave all this stuff?" George asked, pointing at another filing cabinet tipped on its side. Yellowed, wet piles of paperwork covered the floor. "I mean, why didn't Timlico take it with them?"

"Shit, you don't know, do you?"

"Know what?"

"I assumed you knew, but I guess not since you didn't live here back then."

"Well, what happened?"

"There was a freak fire about ten years ago. Some people were killed and the company closed because of the lawsuits."

"Lawsuits? How many people died?"

"Nearly forty."

"Jesus, how?"

Scott pointed the flashlight at a MagCard slot next to a closed office door. "See these panels?"

"Yeah?"

"The doors worked on an electronic passcard system, but when the fire started in the basement, the computer system froze. Apparently, Timlico had used some fly-by-night company out of China for the system and it always had problems. A bunch of people got trapped in their offices while the smoke was sucked through the ventilation ducts. They didn't burn, they suffocated. And then some of the maintenance workers in the basement fucking drowned. They were locked down there and the sprinkler system malfunctioned, filling the room with water."

"Holy shit! How'd the fire start?"

"Some kind of freak accident. It was never explained, I don't think, but I was just a kid, so I don't really remember."

"Damn! This might have been a bad idea."

They had reached the end of the hallway where the door marked MECHANICAL ROOM #7/ BASEMENT ACCESS—RESTRICTED ACCESS awaited them. Looking back, Scott agreed with George. The building was seriously creepy and everything left behind was a reminder that people used to come to this place every morning, never realizing that a day would arrive when they wouldn't go home alive. They felt safe in this building, but that feeling had been a lie. Death was waiting, biding his time, and the Timlico employees were oblivious until it was too late.

"Do you want to go back? I can handle it myself," Scott said, even though he really didn't want to continue alone.

"No, let's just get it done."

Scott nodded and opened the door to reveal a narrow set of concrete stairs leading down to another door. He and George exchanged a look, but they said nothing as they descended, both of them gripping the railing tighter than they would ever admit. The metal was cold and rough.

Scott opened the door at the bottom of the stairs, the hinges squealing from disuse. He reached inside and found a light switch. Several yellowed fluorescent bulbs throughout the basement grudgingly sparked to life, but many did not.

The space was much larger than Scott had expected. Hundreds of steel posts supported the offices above. Endless pipes and metal ducts criss-crossed the ceiling, and the few flickering lights produced a million shifting shadows, creating an unsettling effect, like there were tiny movements everywhere in your peripheral vision.

Just inside the doorway were benches and lockers for the maintenance crew. A broken television with twisted rabbit ears lay on the floor next to a fungus-covered milk crate.

Beyond the lockers were hundreds of desks, filing cabinets, and conference tables, and after that was a graveyard of forgotten office equipment including ancient computers, printers, copiers, and fax machines. The building managers for Timlico had apparently been pack rats. Everything was saved, just in case.

On the far side of the basement were metal stairs leading to a landing and a door marked GENERATOR ROOM. That was where they needed to go, but Scott couldn't make himself take the first step.

There was water on the floor, and that troubled him for reasons he couldn't articulate. A chill crawled across his flesh. Shivering, he wanted to turn back, but how would he explain that to Mary? He didn't check on the generator because he got scared of the dark? There was some spooky water on the floor? He'd never hear the end of it, not if he lived to be a hundred.

"What do you think?" George asked, studying the basement from over Scott's shoulder.

"I think we'd better do what we came to do."

Scott stepped through the doorway and onto the concrete floor, his work boots sending little ripples of water in every direction. The water wasn't deep, but still, he didn't like it being there. Maybe because people had drowned in this room once.

They started walking, glancing into the lockers that had belonged to the maintenance crew. Most of the doors were hanging open. A few still contained moldy clothing on hangers and there were family photos taped inside a couple of others. One locker still had a lunchbox sitting on the top shelf, undisturbed since the morning of the fire.

Scott and George continued onward. After a couple of minutes, the water had reached the top of their boots and slithered down inside, soaking their socks. The sensation was revolting.

"What the hell?" Scott asked. "Is this water getting deeper?"

"Seems like it. Maybe the floor is sloped?"

"Christ, I hope not too much."

Soon they were slipping on rotting papers and other things they couldn't see below the water's black, slimy surface. They touched the timeworn and scarred office furniture as they passed, as if to confirm it was real. Next they were into the land of forgotten computers. There were more than enough Packard Bells, Acers, Dells, and eMachines to stock a few hundred Radio Shacks just in time for Christmas 1998. The monitors were bulky yet the screens were tiny compared to what Scott and George were accustomed to working on.

They weren't too far from the stairs to the generator room when the working overhead lights died without warning.

"Shit," Scott muttered. He lifted the flashlight, shining it on George.

"Let's go back," George said. "I hate the dark."

"Why didn't you say that when I asked?"

"I didn't know it would be *this* dark!"

"The generator room isn't much further," Scott said, pointing the light at the stairs. "Let's get the generator started and then we'll haul ass out of here. We'll be quick."

George didn't look convinced, but he started moving again. Scott did his best to keep the narrow circle of light focused on their goal, but something was wrong. The air was growing colder and heavier. The water had also gotten deeper. It was to their knees and he couldn't recall when that had happened. Then he realized the water was still rising, reaching his waist within seconds.

There was a splash behind them. Scott whirled around, waving the flashlight high and low, left and right, but he saw nothing.

From the darkness came an anguished moan. Then there was another. And then another. Soft at first, then getting louder. None of the sounds seemed real.

Scott opened his mouth to say something, but his lungs filled with smoke. He coughed and gasped. Suddenly there was very little clean air to be had. Thick ribbons of smoke wafted along the top of the water and encircled him like a python.

"Let's go!" George said, diving toward the stairs. Scott followed, coughing and struggling to keep the flashlight out of the water, the circle of light swinging wildly.

The two men hustled up the stairs to the door marked GENERATOR ROOM. Scott pointed the flashlight back to where the waves from their panicked swim were still spreading across the water.

There was no smoke and no one in sight. The basement was silent again, except for the sound of water dripping from their soaked clothes onto the metal landing.

"What the hell was that?" George asked, his words turning to fog in the chilly air.

"I have no fucking clue," Scott replied. "I want to say our imaginations got away from us. Can you believe that? I want to believe it."

"That wasn't my imagination. Something's very wrong. We need to keep moving. Try the door."

Scott did. The door opened without issue. He searched the generator room with his flashlight before entering, just to be safe. For some reason he had expected to find a small generator like the one at his father's hunting cabin, but instead there was a control panel that NASA might have used to launch rockets in the '60s and a wide metal door labeled: RESTRICTED AREA! ACCESS TO BACK-UP GENERATORS 1 THRU 5! AUTHORIZED MECHANICS ONLY.

Scott approached the workstation. There were gauges, buttons, switches, knobs, and a few tiny, blank screens. None of the controls made much sense to him, but there *was* a green button labeled ON. Scott pushed it.

Nothing happened. No sputtering. No revving of power. None of the gauge needles even twitched.

"Damn. Should have figured as much, I guess."

"Broken?" George asked, flipping a few switches as if that might help.

"Something like that. Maybe no fuel. Or maybe I just don't know how to run this thing, ya know?"

"Okay, we tried. Let's get the hell out of here, okay?"

Scott returned to the door, but he stopped dead in his tracks as fear tightened around his throat like a noose. The stairs were being submerged by quickly rising water. Yet that wasn't what made a shriek escape his throat before he knew it was coming.

They weren't alone.

Smoke filled the basement, and in the smoke were shadowy forms moving toward the stairs, their arms flailing above their heads. Forgotten cries and screams bounced off the ceiling, the ducts, the foaming water.

This isn't right, he thought, his mind going numb while trying to process what his eyes were showing him. *This isn't right!*

That was when Scott discovered he couldn't move, couldn't remember how to walk. It was as if his body was an unfamiliar foreign land in which he was trapped behind enemy lines. He urged himself to *move, move, move,* and yet nothing happened.

The smoke figures were closing in. The first of them stumbled at the bottom of the stairs. Scott's eyes were wide as his brain kept sending fervent signals to flee that his body simply ignored.

"Holy mother of God," George whispered, grabbing onto Scott's shoulder to steady himself.

The paralysis broke. He turned, pushed George back into the generator room, and slammed the door shut. The flashlight slipped from his hand and the bulb shattered when it skidded across the floor. Instant blackness washed over the two men as boots clanked on the stairs outside the door.

"What the hell is going on?" Scott said, his voice cracking. "I mean, seriously, what the fuck!"

"I think... I think they're ghosts."

"Ghosts aren't real!"

"Maybe you should tell them that."

Scott stared into the pure black nothingness of the room as the shouts continued outside. Angry hands pounded on the door, scratched at the door-knob. Hoarse screaming followed. Water slipped under the door like a thief and lapped at their boots. Every beat of Scott's heart was a jackhammer pounding his ribs.

This isn't right, he thought, *this isn't right, this isn't right, this isn't right.*

His mind spun and he couldn't stop the words repeating in his head. *This isn't right.*

His head began to ache from the pressure, as if his skull might crack open.

This isn't right!

Esto está todo mal.

This isn't right!

Esto está todo mal.

This isn't right!

The words were all-consuming, but then he realized they weren't just *his* thoughts. He was hear-ing different voices. Men, women, young, old. Some in English, some in Spanish. Strangers in the dark gathered together by the unknown hand of death.

Then came a moment of surreal clarity.

This isn't right.

His first thought when he saw the people in the smoke had been the same thought the workers had when they realized they weren't going home again. They perished repeating those words and now all they could do was forever attempt to escape the inescapable. But they weren't *real,* and that was what mattered.

"I don't think they can hurt us!" Scott said.

George didn't speak right away. Then he whispered: "We're not alone."

Deliberate, wet footsteps approached them. There was a distinct *click, click, click* that reminded Scott of all the times he had mindlessly played with his lighter, flicking at the sparkwheel, causing the flames to jump.

Click, click, click...

The footsteps were getting closer. More clicks. A spark briefly split the darkness.

Click, click, click...

"We have to get out of this room," Scott said, fear overwhelming him. There was another spark, even closer. He stammered, cleared his throat, and forced the words: "Those things out there, I don't think they can hurt us. But whatever's in here..."

"Let's go then, let's go fast," George whispered, directly into Scott's ear, nearly causing him to shriek with fright.

They pulled the door open, stepped onto the landing where the smoky shapes of dead people raged, and dove blindly over the steps. They hit the water hard and began to swim, coughing and choking and splashing. Their arms and legs collided with objects in the water, but they pushed through the darkness threatening to swallow them whole.

After a while, they had no idea which way they were headed, but they kept moving. The smoke was smothering, the water was freezing, and there was heat above them, as if the ceiling were on fire but shedding no light.

They pushed on, side by side, gasping for air and swimming, their hands and arms sometimes colliding.

Then suddenly George was gone.

Scott stopped. His feet settled on the floor. The water was up to his chest, but that didn't tell him where he was. He remained very still and listened. The screams were muffled and distant, and the smoke wasn't as bad here.

"George?" Scott whispered. "Where the hell are you?"

There was movement to his right. Something broke the surface, splashing wildly. Then silence. Then more splashing and a wordless scream ending in a wet squeal as George vanished underneath again.

Scott moved in that direction and a flailing hand grabbed his arm under the water. He yelped in surprise but clutched the hand with both of his, pulling as hard as he could. He felt the resistance of the water as if a substantial weight were being lifted and then he heard another splash followed by coughing and gasping as George surfaced.

"Something pulled me under," George cried, spitting, choking. "Something so *cold!*"

He didn't wait for Scott to reply and he didn't take a moment to catch his breath. He started swimming again, more frantically than before, and Scott followed, not wanting to meet the cold thing that had grabbed George under the dark water.

Soon their hands struck the floor. They stumbled to their feet and ran, the water sloshing around their knees as they smacked into furniture and equipment. They still had no idea where they were, but now the water was only ankle deep.

They kept running blind, and Scott pulled slightly ahead of George just in time to slam into the maintenance crew's lockers. He howled, the metal edges pushing hard into his flesh. George crashed into the locker next to him with a dense thud and a hiss of pain.

Scott staggered backwards, holding his face with both hands as if to squeeze the agony away, and he muttered curses that would have made a sailor blush. He didn't know how long he stood like that in the dark but finally the worst of the pain dulled enough for him to think straight.

"Come on, I know where we are!" Scott said.

He used the lockers as a guide to locate the door where they had entered the basement. They rushed up the stairs, their soaked clothes weighing heavily on them, and Scott shoved the door to the hallway open without slowing down. He stumbled and hit the opposite wall hard, collapsing as the last of his energy was sapped from his legs. George tripped as he passed through the doorway and landed on the mildewed floor next to Scott, gasping in short breaths.

The door slowly closed behind them.

Scott and George lay there, stunned and exhausted, as the storm raged against the ceiling above them and their heartbeats echoed in their ears. Time passed. Part of Scott expected the door to fly open to reveal some monster charging after them, but nothing happened. They were alone in the hallway again.

"Jesus H. Christ," Scott whispered. "Let's get the hell out of this place and never come back."

They pushed themselves to their feet and didn't stop moving again until they passed through the double doors at the end of the hallway, where they stopped only long enough for Scott to slam the doors shut. Then they crossed the warehouse and made their way to the loading docks. Mary was on the other end of the building and Scott had no idea what he would tell her when she returned, other than maybe how goddamned happy he was to be alive.

He stepped out onto the dock plate and turned his head up toward the storm. Lightning flashed, thunder rumbled, and rain pelted his face, but everything about the moment was revitalizing. The clean rain was a godsend after being in that disgusting basement water. Deep down he felt like he had been born again. He realized he was crying.

"George, I believe we're two very, very lucky guys," Scott said as he wiped the rain from his face.

When George didn't reply, Scott turned to ask if he was okay, but the words never left his lips.

George stood in the shadows near the loading dock, his head tilted down and his chin resting on his chest.

This isn't right.

His thumb flicked at the sparkwheel of a silver lighter—*click, click, click*—until a flame jumped to life in the darkness.

When George's cold eyes rose to meet Scott's gaze, Scott wanted to scream but he couldn't. Besides, he knew screaming wouldn't help him now. Screaming wouldn't help at all.

This isn't right.

Scott had learned an important lesson from the shadowy ghosts in the smoke, the echoes of the workers whose deaths were seared into the memory of the building. Screaming wouldn't open locked doors, it wouldn't extinguish flames, it wouldn't stop rising water, and it certainly wouldn't prevent whatever terrible horror was about to transpire.

As death approached from the darkness, Scott also realized something else.

George had found what they left behind.

STORY NOTES

BY BRIAN JAMES FREEMAN

SOME READERS ARE INTERESTED IN story notes from the author at the end of a short story collection, so this section exists for them. Feel free to skip this part if that sort of thing isn't your cup of tea, though.

That said, for those of you who enjoy a little inside information from the author about how the work came to be, stories *can* still be spoiled if you dive into the notes first.

If you've arrived here before reading the rest of the book, please do kindly flip back to the introduction or first story without further ado. Thank you!

MORE THan MIDNIGHT

✕

THE ENTIRE STORY ARC OF "Pop-Pop" arrived like a tactical nuke while I was waiting in the drive-thru line for my breakfast sandwich at a fast food restaurant. The experience was like watching a short film inside my head: starting with the teenage twins and their mom standing in the living room, to the discovery in the attic, all the way to Gram-Gram's revelation at the end. Because I'm not a natural at writing, I messed up the execution on my first attempt and the story required a few dozen revisions to get right, but I love how the final draft came together.

✕

"ANSWERING THE CALL" IS ONE of my favorites in this collection even though I know it isn't my best. That might sound strange, but the story was inspired by the memory of a family friend saving the family's answering machine tape (remember those?) because it contained her recently deceased mother's outgoing message. She wanted to be able to hear her mom's voice again and that answering machine provided a way.

The cool thing about this story's publication history is it was the *second* story I submitted to Tom and Elizabeth Monteleone for *Borderlands 5*. The first story wasn't working for them. I tried three or four drafts and it just wouldn't click.

But I wanted to sell a story to the *Borderlands* series, dammit, so in a fit of inspiration, I wrote "Answering the Call" instead and sent that. Tom and Elizabeth loved it and only asked for one change. The original title was "Answering the Call of the Dead" and, as they correctly pointed out, that title would have robbed the story of much of its power.

IN THE SUMMER OF 2000, I was home from my sophomore year of college and mowing the lawn when some guys drove by and threw a beer bottle at me. They missed; the story "The Final Lesson" landed. Brian Keene bought this one for the old *Horrorfind* website, back when publishing fiction online was still a relatively new idea. The title then was "Bigger and Better," which I liked, but "The Final Lesson" fits the themes considerably better.

✕

"LOVING ROGER" SPARKED THE ONE face-to-face conversation I had with Richard Laymon. This was at Brian Keene's house while I was in college. I had no idea what to actually say to Dick, so I basically hid in the corner, like I usually do, and said nothing. Finally, I gathered the courage to speak with him, still unsure of what I should actually say, and I ended up talking about the first thing to pop into my head: a paper I had written for one of my journalism classes the previous semester.

The class was about writing feature news articles, but the final assignment was something kind of different. The professor told us to imagine a wife driving home with a surprise for her husband. We were to describe the drive and the surprise, using as many details as we could, "kind of like a short story."

I wrote "Loving Roger" based on the assignment prompt and I'm guessing it was unlike anything anyone else in the class came up with. I'm still not sure why I actually took the approach I did, given the subject matter and how old and conservative the professor was. The idea was just *there,* so I ran with it like I normally would when I had an idea for a story.

After I turned the paper in, it wasn't very long before I had second thoughts. Sure, my take on the topic was what came naturally to me, but had that *really* been a good idea for this particular class?

When I received my paper back, I immediately saw all of the red ink at the top of the first page and my heart dropped. Then I read what the professor had written:

"I don't understand what you've done here, but it's VERY creative. A+"

I passed the class.

So, not knowing what else to say, I told Richard Laymon this story there in Brian Keene's dining room and then I asked him: "Is that a good sign or a bad sign?"

Dick thought about it for a long moment and replied: "I think that's the *best* sign."

Everyone laughed, and I was relieved and thrilled to meet one of my heroes and not make too much of an ass of myself, even though in hindsight I have absolutely *no idea* what my question meant.

✕

"AMONG US" WOULD HAVE APPEARED on a website I ran in 1999 and 2000 called Dueling Minds if I hadn't shut down the experiment before the next issue was due to be posted. The "webzine" featured work from some incredible authors and artists, and was a lot of fun to put together, but I simply ran out of time in my schedule to work on it.

Each issue featured four or five stories inspired by the same piece of artwork, giving readers the chance to glimpse how the imaginations of these different authors worked. (Later on, I'd use the same idea for an anthology called *Dueling Minds,* which was published in the Cemetery Dance Signature Series.)

I no longer have the artwork that served as the inspiration for "Among Us" but I clearly remember it involved a face inside a man's glowing chest. I think the story is fun, if pretty different from what I focus on these days.

Also, huge thanks go out to Allen K for giving this one a home in his *Inhuman* magazine, along with some great new artwork to boot.

STORY NOTES

✕

"NOT WITHOUT REGRETS" STARTED LIFE as part of a novel and was later published as a standalone chapbook by Cemetery Dance Publications in 2004 under the title "Pulled Into Darkness." Almost everything in the version of the story that appears in this collection is different, though. I slashed 4,000 words during the most recent edit and rewrite, changed the characters and their dynamics, and generally left nothing the same except for the overarching premise. But I like this approach better, so here we are.

✕

THE OPENING SCENARIO IN "WHAT They Left Behind" is fairly close to something that happened to me in real life. In the early 2000s, my father-in-law was moving his logistics business into an abandoned IBM office building. Not because his company was failing like the one in the story, but because business was booming and he needed more space.

The only facility available that met his needs was this old office building, which required a ton of demolition work. We spent weeks gutting the offices and conference rooms to convert the structure into a proper warehouse, but before the demo work began, I gave myself a private tour of the abandoned hallways and offices, of course.

It wasn't as creepy as the building in "What They Left Behind," but it certainly wasn't a place I'd want to spend the night.

HERE WE ARE NOW, AT the end of the collection. Thanks again for joining me on this visit to these stories set in a world where it's always later than midnight. Until the next time we meet, be careful when you venture into the mysterious dark places inside yourself....

SPECIAL THANKS FOR PATREON SUPPORTERS

THE FOLLOWING PEOPLE GENEROUSLY SUP-PORTED my Patreon page as of August 1, 2018 and made this new expanded edition possible. My deepest thanks go out to:

Vicki Liebowitz, Michael Fowler, Shanon Cole, Brian Freeman, Louis Toth, Donald Shelton, Matt Schwartz, Doug Clegg, Mark Sieber, Dez Nemec, Patrick Bishop, Paul Fry, Richard A. Shirley, Keith Prochaska, Brian Keene, Robert Voss, Deborah Naus, Earl Robinson, Susan Pearson, Steven McDonald, Robin Bruner, Todd Nesbitt, Julie H. Sullivan,

Debra Torma, Adam Harding-Jones, Ethan Harris, Jonathan Sweet, Michelle Rother Lindsay, Thomas Millman, Russell King, Aaron Cohen, Pamela Taylor, Tami Franzel, David Jensen, Lisa Von Pervieux, Ann Waters, Robin Trischmann, Keejia M. Houchin, Alan Caldwell, Joseph Cameli, David F. Sabol, Rockie Suttle, Matthew Williams, Richard Platt, David Zicherman, Ron Weekes, James Coniglio, David Lars Chamberlain, John Fahey, Darren Heil, Kris Van Der Sande, Stephen Bamberg, Christa Jennings, Dan Newman, Roxane McLarnan Geggie, J Rivers Walsh, Elena DeGarmo, Bryan Moose, Dodi Miller, Todd Houts, Robert S. Righetti, Robert Mingee, Linda Przygoda, Veronica Ukas, Lisa A. Toombs, Jason Sechrest, Jason Canny, Lori Adams, Chris Nauta, Martha J. Davis, Sean Strange, Lori Reynolds, John J. Questore, Tami Kietzmann, Susan J. Darling, Michael Sauers, Gary L. Phillips, David Greenlaw, Twikie Simms, Ross W. Davidson, Rich DeMars, Larry Kinney, Michelle Floyd, Harold Dean Cook II, Deanna Kubisty, Janice Hill, Dorothy Lewis, Anderson Yee, Brian Nicola, Martin Garcia, David Pagan, Ronda Pennington, Daniel Zacharski, Philip

Special Thanks

Wickstrand, Joel McCandless, David McClung, Shannan Ross, Sue Wilson, Kim Meier-Carroll, David Ray, David Kipp, Kerry McKenna, Pamela A. Abel, Gary St. Clair, Keith Fritz, Heather Sage, Dominick, Steve Rider, Sean McBride, Levana Taylor, Michael Gutierrez, Connie Harrison, Shelly McGhan, Lynne Heinmiller, Kristy Lytle, Roger Terry, Kevin F. Wilson, Mary Grace Panebianco, Michael John Pawly, Susan Gray, Marilyn K. Barber, Hunter Shea, Edward Roads, Stephen Herman, Ron Reese, Robert Brouhard, Tabitha Brouhard, Brad Saenz.

IF YOU WOULD LIKE TO learn more about the special rewards I'm creating for my readers, please visit this page:

https://www.patreon.com/BrianJamesFreeman

Do you love
short stories full of
DARK TWISTS
AND TURNS?

Support
Brian James
Freeman
on Patreon for new
short stories, novel excerpts,
and much more!

Some supporters even qualify
for exclusive Limited Edition books
that will never be reprinted!

Find out more at:
**https://www.patreon.com/
BrianJamesFreeman**

Thank you!

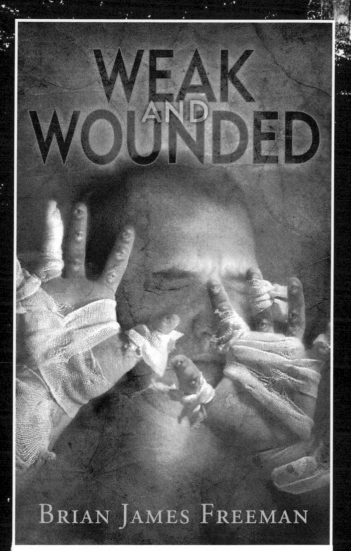

LOST AND LONELY
BRIAN JAMES FREEMAN
Learn more at
BrianJamesFreeman.com

DREAMLIKE STATES

BRIAN JAMES FREEMAN

Learn more at
BrianJamesFreeman.com

Made in the USA
Middletown, DE
07 May 2019